W9-BCU-659

SCRUB DOG
OF ALASKA

Other Books by Walt Morey

SCRUB DOG OF ALASKA

by Walt Morey

E. P. Dutton & Co., Inc. New York

c.1
H-1972

Published simultaneously in Canada by Clarke,
Irwin & Company Limited, Toronto and Vancouver

SBN: 0-525-38908-3 LCC: 73-157954

Designed by Dorothea von Elbe
Printed in the U.S.A.
First Edition

To Rosalind,
who believed in this one from the first

-1-

The whole mining community of Aurora named the pup. At first, when they were annoyed by something he'd done, they said, "That no-good scrub of Smiley Jackson's." But that was too long. They shortened it to "That Scrub!" which was the lowest form of no good. And Jackson agreed with them.

Jackson considered himself an expert. He was choosing pups to build a new team. He raised, trained, and ran dogs in the Alaska sled-dog races. He studied each carefully, idly fingering the ugly scar on his cheek which pulled his lips upward into a gargoyle-like smile. He noted each pup's disposition, agility, alertness, and especially its courage. He'd already chosen the black pup Keno for his leader. But the wolf-gray scrub showed no promise that he would ever make a good sled dog. To Jackson he wasn't worth even a bullet. He took an ax to do the job and approached quietly from the rear.

Some instinct warned the pup. He glanced back— and leaped sideways. The swing threw Jackson off

1

balance and he sprawled in the snow. The ax flew from his hands. The handle smacked the pup in the ribs, and he yelped in surprise and pain. Before Jackson could get up the pup raced into the trees and disappeared.

Jackson could easily have followed the pup and disposed of him. But now that the dog was gone he would no longer have to be fed. That was all that mattered. It was winter. In all probability the pup would starve or freeze to death, or fall prey to some hungry predator. In fact, he might be dead by morning. It was twenty below now, and the temperature would plunge lower as the night advanced.

But Jackson failed to take into account that there was wolf blood in this young dog's veins. The wild instinct for survival had been bred into him for generations. Now it came to the fore as the cold and hungry pup struggled off through the snow toward the cluster of houses a half mile away.

Within an hour the pup found frozen table scraps in a garbage pile behind a house. They were hard to chew with his baby teeth, but he managed. At another house he watched from the protection of a bush as a man hung a sack containing meat on a nail of his back porch. When the man disappeared inside, the dog crept forward and looked longingly up at the sack. The sweet odor of fresh meat hung on the frigid air. Saliva ran in the pup's mouth. He licked his lips hungrily.

There was an empty box on the porch under the sack. He jumped onto the box and reared up against

2

the wall, trying to reach the sack. His clawing at the wall brought an immediate rush of steps toward the door. He jumped from the box, fell clumsily, and rolled off the steps. A hole appeared under the porch before his nose. He had barely scrambled into the inner gloom when the door opened. Feet tramped about in the snow. The man muttered to himself angrily, then went back inside.

The pup worked his way farther under the house and found warmth. The stove just over his head warmed the floor, which in turn brought warmth down to him. He spent a very comfortable night.

But for the lucky accident of diving under the porch, Scrub might have frozen to death.

The next morning he returned to Jackson's one-room cabin. Jackson was outside feeding the pups and saw him coming. He grabbed a stick and ran at him, shouting. Scrub fled back into the brush. By now ravenously hungry.

He returned to Aurora and visited the garbage pile. This time there was no food. He wandered among the other houses, found garbage piles with a few bites of food, and eked out a slim meal. The day was biting cold.

He went to the house where he'd spent the previous night. A man was outside cutting wood. When Scrub approached, he picked up a stick, hurled it at him, and shouted angrily, "Get outa here! Beat it!" The stick missed. Scrub ran away again. He had learned the most important lesson to his survival: man was to be avoided.

He slunk about searching for a warm place to hole up. He discovered another house he could get under. The hole was at the back where there were no doors or windows to give away his approach. By being careful, he could come and go with little fear of detection.

In succeeding days Scrub found an old shed with a pile of dried grass in a corner. Best of all, he later stumbled onto an abandoned mine test-hole. It was dark inside and the air smelled stale. But down in the earth he was completely protected from the weather— and man didn't come here. Food remained his biggest problem.

Stealth and cunning were part of his heritage. Pup though he was, clumsy and awkward, necessity forced him to become sly and clever. In time he learned to visit the garbage piles only at night. He learned that the back porches of houses were good places to watch. Housewives sometimes put hot dishes out to cool or freeze and his delicate nose led him unerringly. Some porches had plain wooden boxes that served as refrigerators in which food was kept fresh. Sometimes a box was not tightly closed. More often than not he found it.

Soon Scrub was automatically blamed when food was missed or a food box was broken into. Often he was innocent. Other families had young dogs which ran free during their first months. They formed into a pack and stole whenever the opportunity arose. But since they were fed fairly regularly, they were seldom

4

blamed. Scrub grew surprisingly on his lean, uncertain diet. But he was never the fat, roly-poly pup the others were.

Scrub's sides were thin, his thick gray coat matted. Young as he was, the wolf in him was becoming visible in his black-masked face. His nose lengthened. His jaws became wider, showing the promise of tremendous crushing strength. His eyes changed to amber and he had a wolf's trick of tilting his head down slightly and looking obliquely up at any object that caught his attention. His legs became longer, the bones heavy. His front feet seemed out of proportion to the rest of his body. He became particularly clever at dodging sticks or other missiles.

Someone might have shot him, but he still was Smiley Jackson's property. Such an act might have aroused Jackson's hair-trigger temper. He was a vindictive man and, in this small community, no one wanted to risk his wrath. So they tolerated Scrub and ran him off whenever he approached. The teeth of every dog and the hand of every man, woman, and child in Aurora was set against him—except one.

David Martin was a young, slender boy about fourteen. He had dark eyes and straight black hair. His smooth skin was neither light nor dark, but something of an in-between olive. He went to the little one-room school with the rest of the Aurora kids. After school he hiked off alone through the settlement, carrying lunch bucket and books. He entered a trail in the snow that led through the trees.

The first time the boy came upon him, Scrub was trying to dig a rabbit from a burrow in the frozen earth. If he caught the rabbit it would be his first food in several days. He was industriously tearing at the hard earth when he heard the crunch of snow and jerked his head up. The boy stood a few feet off. Scrub started backing away, prepared to run. He knew what to expect. He was ready to dodge the moment the boy's arm would draw back to throw.

Instead, the boy spoke to him, "You look awful thin. I'll bet you're hungry." His voice was gentle and quiet. The dog stopped, ears pricked forward, listening. The boy advanced slowly, opening his lunch box. He held forth a sandwich, "Here, I couldn't eat all my lunch." Scrub knew it was food and saliva ran in his mouth. He licked his lips hungrily. But he could not let the boy come close. He kept backing away.

The pack of free-running dogs, led by the black Keno, came trotting through the snow. They spotted Scrub and started forward on a run. Keno was in the lead. The boy snatched up a stick and Scrub bolted away. He glanced over his shoulder as he ran, ready to dodge when the stick was thrown. The boy was turned, facing the advancing pack. He hurled the stick at them. It caught Keno in the side and brought a yelp of surprise and pain. The black dog turned tail and raced back toward Aurora with the pack at his heels.

Scrub stopped uncertainly. The boy came toward him again, holding out the sandwich. His voice was low and coaxing, "Come on. It's good. I'm not going to hurt you. Come on."

Scrub listened, looking obliquely up at the boy. He wanted the food desperately. But he could not let the boy advance beyond a certain distance. He began backing off again.

The boy stopped. "All right, I don't blame you for not trusting anybody. Here." He tossed the sandwich in the snow under the dog's nose. For a moment Scrub hesitated, but the aroma of fresh food was too much. He grabbed it and gulped it down, watching the boy carefully.

"You see, I don't want to hurt you," the boy said. "Why should I? I wish I had more to give you. Maybe I'll see you again. Good-bye." He disappeared among the trees.

Scrub didn't see the boy for several nights. When he did, the boy had part of a sandwich and a couple of cookies for him. Again he talked quietly, coaxingly as he held out the food and tried to approach. "You remember me. I gave you a sandwich and chased the other dogs away so you could eat in peace. Here's some more. Come on, come and get it." Once again Scrub could not let the boy advance too close. The boy finally gave up and tossed the sandwich and cookies into the snow. Again he walked away among the trees.

Scrub saw the boy often after that, and more than once the food he received kept him from going hungry. He began to make a point of appearing somewhere near the trail at the edge of the trees where the boy was sure to see him. There was always food for him, and the boy continued to talk quietly. Then one night the boy did not come.

Scrub hung about the spot near the trail day after day. He went into the trees where the boy always disappeared, but found nothing. Day after day he returned, sat in the snow beside the trail, and waited. He missed not only the food he'd come to expect, but the first faint feeling of friendship he'd ever known with a human. The dog in him craved this. A fresh fall of snow finally wiped out all sign of the trail. Then Scrub knew the boy was not coming and gave up waiting. He had to scrounge harder than ever for food now to fill the needs of his growing body.

Gradually the days began to lengthen. The sun swung higher across the blue bowl of the sky. Its brilliance carried the first faint warmth of spring. A chinook blew up from the south and began biting into the snow blanket. The first gray-green patches of tundra appeared. Crocuses pushed through the melting snow and spread their blooms to a softening sky.

Ptarmigans, rabbits, and weasels began to lose their white coats. A host of small animals came from burrows beneath the thinning snow and dashed about in a frantic search for food. They were happy to be out of their winter confines into the wide, big world again.

The river ice became scored and rotten. Water ran along either bank, beneath the ice and over its rough surface. Then one day, with a noise like thunder that brought all Aurora racing to the river bank to view the spectacle, the ice began moving inexorably toward the distant sea.

Birch buds burst along the edge of the woods and the first leaves shone pale green and satiny smooth. Great V's of geese, ducks, and swans began passing over. At times the sky was alive with their talking. A cow moose emerged from the brush followed by her spindly legged calf. They made their way slowly to the ice-free river.

Spring had come to the north.

Scrub entered spring half-starved and ragged. The change of season brought no improvement in his condition. This was not altogether due to the people of Aurora, who hated him and drove him from their houses and garbage piles. The pack of free-running dogs had made his life miserable by chasing him at every opportunity. They were worse with the coming of spring. They were bigger, more aggressive, and they were led by Keno. His special delight was harassing Scrub.

Jackson planned to make Keno the lead dog of his new team. He was all black and sleek from being well-fed. He was exceptionally strong and fast afoot, and he was a little older than Scrub. Keno and the others made a game of chasing Scrub and robbing him of any food he had found or managed to steal. Scrub hunted the nearby woods to add to his slim diet, but wild game

9

was scarce this close to Aurora and the pack was always hunting, too.

Several times Scrub had lain in the fringe of brush near Jackson's cabin and watched, drooling, stomach aching as the musher fed his dogs. He had sneaked up to the cabin in the dead of night in the hope that some morsel had been missed. But Keno slept near the steps and sounded the alarm that brought Jackson cursing to the door with a gun. Twice he had shot at Scrub as the pup raced into the protection of the brush. Both times he missed. Most of Scrub's meager food came from prowling the yards and cabins of Aurora. When he found something, he'd slip into the woods, where he could hide and eat in peace.

Keno knew this and was constantly on the lookout for him. The moment he spotted Scrub with food the race was on, with the whole pack streaming out behind Keno and urged on by anyone who happened to see it. "Take him! Go get him, Keno! Get the no-good thief," they'd shout. Quite often Scrub didn't make the protection of the trees and had to drop his precious food in order to get away. Keno and the pack would stop and devour what he had worked so hard to steal. This happened again and again during the summer, with the result that Scrub added very little weight and muscle at a time he should have been storing it up to see him through the coming winter.

Then one day Scrub stole a haunch of venison from a back porch and was slipping off toward the trees. The pack rounded the corner of a house and Keno spotted him. Keno let out a bellow and gave chase. The pack followed, yapping and barking. Scrub dug out for the woods at full speed. Once there he could dodge about among the trees and try to lose them. But he was hampered by the size of the haunch and Keno gained steadily.

Scrub made the trees, but the black dog was so close that Scrub didn't dare slow up to dodge or twist. He fled straight away trying to outrun them.

Keno gained and soon was snapping at Scrub's flying heels. Scrub could have dropped the meat, raced on, and escaped, as he had done many times. But he hadn't eaten for several days and was ravenously hungry. This time, when he knew he'd be caught, he dropped his prize and whirled, head lowered, teeth bared to fight.

Keno piled straight into him and both dogs reared on hind legs, teeth slashing. For a few seconds the lighter, scrawny Scrub actually held his own with Keno. Then the heavier dog's weight and strength bore him down. Keno straddled Scrub, teeth fastened in his throat. That was the signal for the pack to pile on. They buried Scrub beneath their weight. Now Scrub was fighting for his life. Somehow he twisted from Keno's jaws and with a mighty surge came to his feet, snapping right and left. Then the pack rolled over him again. Teeth tore at his thin body. Keno was at his throat again when blackness closed over him.

A few minutes later the pack trotted out of the woods, tails waving as if nothing had happened. Keno carried the remains of the haunch, which was his right as leader.

The silence of death settled over the forest. In a small sunlit glade the torn-up earth and still, mangled form of a wolf-gray animal was the only evidence of the savage battle that had been fought here.

- 2 -

The sun rode majestically through its high summer arc.
A light shaft filtered through the thick tree branches
and bathed the little glade. A squirrel came cautiously
down a tree trunk and sat up, chattering nervously. A
second followed. They chased each other around the
tree several times, then cut across the glade past the
still form of the dog. A weasel rose out of the grass.
His snake-like head and beady eyes followed the play-
ing squirrels. He darted toward them. He was halfway
across the glade when the dog's head rose from the
ground. The weasel stopped, surprised, then in a wink
he disappeared back into the grass.

The dog lay immovable for some time, as though
gathering strength. Finally he made an effort to rise.
He got his front feet up, and fell on his side. He lay a
few minutes, panting. He tried again. On the third attempt he stood wobbling on three legs, sick and ter-
ribly weak. His right hind-leg hung useless. He tried to
put it down, but the moment it touched the ground he
whimpered in pain. Finally he hobbled off on three

legs. He went straight away from Aurora. The dog struggled ahead for a hundred yards, then his strength gave out, and he lay down.

It was here that Harvey Scott found him.

Scotty, or White-Water Scotty to his friends, lived on a boiling stretch of river thirty miles away. He came striding through the forest, his shock of brown hair blowing in the breeze. Scotty had been a prospector and trapper until he lost his left hand in an accident. A metal hook was now fastened to the stub. He'd given up trapping and had sold his dog team. It was too hard to skin out fur with only one hand. Now he prospected, working the small streams in the area. He admitted he did well.

Two or three times a year Scotty visited Aurora and loaded up with supplies at the trading post. That was as close to a city as he wanted to get. When he became hungry for talk, he hiked up to see his good friends Fred and Celia Martin and their fourteen-year-old son, David. They lived a mile or so out of Aurora. Fred Martin ran one of the longest trap lines in the area. Scotty was on his way to visit them when he came upon the dog.

He squatted on his heels and studied the dog. He noted the rips in its hide, a particularly bad one in the throat, the broken leg. Because he'd had dogs most of his life he could guess what had happened to this one.

"Well, friend," he said gently, "you've been in quite a fight. I'd guess no one dog did this to you. Couldn't

14

you run away or did they corner you?" He stroked the dog with his big hand. The dog looked at him with amber eyes, but did not try to move. "This is no place for you, friend," Scotty continued. "You need help or you're going to die. Let's see what I can do."

Very carefully Scotty worked his hand and the hook under the dog's body. Scrub whimpered. "It's all right, friend," said the soothing voice. "It's all right." With infinite care he lifted the dog and held him against his chest. Then he continued toward the Martins' cabin.

The Martins' neat three-room log cabin squatted in the center of a small meadow. There were two out-buildings, one a food cache high on stilts, the other a place on the ground where Fred Martin stored his furs. Nine sled dogs were staked out around the cabin, each with his own house. They set up a great clamor at the sight of Scotty. The door to the main cabin was open. Scotty called, "Anybody home?"

Without waiting for an answer, he walked into the kitchen. A small, neat woman with straight jet-black hair wound in braids about her head turned from the stove. A boy of about fourteen, with the same fine-boned features and smooth olive skin as the woman, sat in a chair. A pair of homemade crutches lay on the floor beside him. Mother and son chorused, "Scotty! Scotty! Come in!"

The boy said, "Hey, a dog! Where'd you find him? What's wrong with him?"

Scotty laid the dog carefully on the kitchen floor and

15

said, "He got chewed up in a fight. He can't walk. I couldn't leave him to die. You got any hot water and rags, Celia?"

Celia hurried to get them. The boy leaned forward and looked at the dog intently. "I know him. I saw him almost every night on the way home from school last winter. He always looked half-starved."

"He's half-starved now," Scotty said. "You can count every rib."

Celia returned with rags and a basin of hot water. Scotty began washing the dog. Scrub lay perfectly still, flinching only when the man touched a particularly bad spot. When Scotty cleansed the gaping tear in his throat, he whimpered.

"He's pretty brave to take that pain," David said admiringly.

"He knows I'm trying to help him." Scotty finished the washing and asked, "You got a sharp needle and thread, Celia? We'll have to sew up these worst rips. You can do the sewing."

"I've never sewn anything but cloth or leather, Scotty."

"I'll show you what to do."

They worked on the dog for over an hour. He endured patiently, even when Celia sewed the bad tear in his throat. When she finished, she stroked his head and murmured, "It's all over now. You were very brave."

Under Scotty's direction, David whittled splints for the broken leg. With Celia's help the prospector pulled

16

the bones together. She held the splints and helped bind them tight to the leg. Afterward they moved Scrub onto an old blanket, and Scotty pulled him into a corner of the kitchen, where he would be out of the way. The sun had dropped beneath the distant rim of trees. Dusk shadowed the kitchen.

Celia lit the lamp.

Scotty leaned back and sighed, "You did fine, Celia. That's the biggest sewing job I've ever done on a dog."

"Where did you find him?" Celia asked.

"In the woods, about half a mile from Aurora." He studied the dog critically. "He's a young one, a last-winter's pup. He's got the makings of a big, powerful dog. Look at the size of those leg bones and feet, the depth of his chest. Got some wolf in him, too. A quarter, maybe a little more. He'd be a pretty fair-looking dog if he was fed up and cared for. Wonder why anybody'd let him go to pot like this?" He glanced at the boy. "You said you'd seen him, Davie. What's the story on him?"

"He's a cull that Smiley Jackson threw out. He was always sneaking around houses trying to steal something to eat. Everybody hated him. They called him Scrub. I used to feed him what I had left in my lunch bucket."

"What you deliberately saved to feed him," Celia said.

"He always looked so starved."

"Scrub." Scotty shook his head. "Not much of a name to live up to."

"You said he could be a pretty good dog," Celia said. "Then why did Jackson cull him? What makes him a scrub, Scotty?"

"I don't know. I wouldn't have culled him on the strength of what I see here. Maybe what's wrong with this dog is Smiley Jackson."

"What do you mean?"

"Jackson thinks he knows it all when it comes to dogs. But he's always selling dogs to other mushers, who then use them to beat him in races. Maybe he made a mistake judging this one, too. When this dog was little, I'll bet he was so clumsy he fell all over himself. A big clumsy pup never looks too bright. Maybe Jackson didn't take any of that into consideration."

"We've got to notify him his dog is here," Celia said.

"Why?" David demanded.

"Because it's his dog."

David looked at the dog lying on the blanket, unable to move, enduring pain without a murmur. A great sympathy welled up in him. "Jackson threw him out when he was a little fellow. He could have frozen to death, starved, or been killed by some big animal. I used to see him sneaking around scrounging for enough to live, being chased by the other dogs, people throwing things at him. He's had enough trouble."

"I feel sorry for him too," Celia said. "But Jackson is mean enough to try to cause trouble for us if he found out he was here and we hadn't told him."

"If we send him back, Jackson'll knock him in the head for sure," David warned.

"That would be Jackson for you," Scotty agreed.

Celia frowned, biting a fingernail thoughtfully. "Scotty, wouldn't you like a dog? You live far enough away so Jackson would never see him."

Scotty shook his head. "Had dogs for twenty-five years and loved every one of 'em. Doctored 'em when they got sick, patched 'em up when they got hurt, and buried 'em when they died. I don't need 'em now and I don't want to go through that again."

"A dog would be a companion."

"When I feel lonesome and want talk I hike up here and pester you folks," Scotty said. "I'm sorry. By the way, where is Fred?"

"He left three days ago to almost rebuild one of the overnight cabins a grizzly wrecked. He figured it would take almost a week. I'm glad you came." Celia smiled. "Fred didn't cut enough wood. I'm about out. David can't handle the chain saw or ax with that broken leg."

"I'll take care of it first thing in the morning," Scotty said. "But it's gonna cost you dinner and a lot of talk."

"Dinner first," Celia said. "Then talk. What would you like, Scotty?"

David knew what was coming. His mother and Scotty went through this little ritual every time he came.

Scotty scratched his head thoughtfully. "You got any bacon?"

19

"We've been saving a piece," Celia smiled.

"We could have bacon pancakes," Scotty suggested. "That all right with you and Davie?" Pancakes with diced pieces of bacon in the batter for flavor were Scotty's special treat.

"It's fine," Celia said.

"What're we going to do about the dog, about Scrub?" David asked.

"Nothing. Your father will decide when he comes home."

"Dad won't let us keep him."

"Probably not. We don't need another dog. But he can make that decision."

Scotty went out to wash and bring in the slab of bacon. David watched his mother move about the kitchen and wondered if he would ever get around like that again. Now that he was on crutches he seemed more conscious of her light, quick steps. His father had laughingly said she was as fast as a squirrel because she didn't weigh much more. For all her slightness David knew she was surprisingly strong and capable. She had been educated at the mission school and had worked two years in one of the big stores in Anchorage before marrying Fred Martin and moving out here. Except for Nick and Jean Moore, David's parents associated very little with the people of the settlement. His father was a trapper. He had little in common with the miners of Aurora.

The dog moved a bit and sighed. David's thoughts

20

returned to the dog. He was still thinking about him when Scotty came in with the slab of bacon. David asked, "Scotty, will the dog get well?"

"Sure. Those rips in his hide look worse than they are."

"But his leg's broken."

"It'll mend." Scotty began dicing bacon, holding the slab in place with his hook. "He'll be as good as ever."

"How can you be sure?"

Scotty glanced at him. "Broken bones heal. You know that. There's no reason this dog's shouldn't."

"The leg's going to be stiff and sore and weak," David said thoughtfully. "Every time he puts it down the pain's going to be awful." He was aware his mother had turned her head and was listening.

"It'll hurt," Scotty agreed. "It's a broken bone. But when the time comes to walk he'll endure the pain. He instinctively knows he's got to try to use it or the leg will never get strong enough to walk again."

"How can he, when it'll hurt so much?"

"He's an animal and can't reason. He does what nature tells him to do." Scotty gave Celia a double handful of diced bacon. She spread it in the frying pan, where it began to sizzle. Scotty turned then and looked at David. "Speaking of walking. How come you're still on crutches? I figured you'd be off them by now."

"He should be." Celia didn't look up. "The leg is healed. The doctor took the crutches away the last time we were in and told David to start walking."

"Why didn't you?" Scotty asked.

"It's not strong enough," David insisted. "I can tell. I could fall and break it again. Then it might never heal. And it hurts. If you knew how much it hurt just to try to straighten it or touch it to the ground."

"That's really the whole thing." Celia poured the diced bacon into the batter and began beating it. Her voice was half-angry. "It hurts, so David won't even try. When we got back from the doctor's the last time, he sat in that chair for almost a week and refused to move because he didn't have his crutches. We coaxed, threatened, tried to reason. But it did no good. Fred finally made him those crutches so he'd get outside for a little exercise and fresh air."

They'd been over this many times and David had only one answer. He gave it again. "When I know I can walk, I will."

"How'll you ever know if you don't try?" Scotty asked.

"That's exactly what we've been telling him." Celia poured batter into the pan.

"You sound like I don't want to walk."

"We're beginning to wonder, David."

"Naturally it'll hurt when you first start walking," Scotty reasoned. "You haven't used those leg muscles for months. It's the muscles that'll hurt. They're weak and flabby and sort of kinked up now because you keep your knee bent. The longer you wait, the weaker that leg'll become and the more it'll hurt when you do try to use it."

"The doctor made that clear to him," Celia said. "But it did no good. As a matter of fact, we've about come to the conclusion that David may become a permanent invalid, simply because he broke a leg and now hasn't the courage to try to walk on it when it's healed."

Scotty looked at David soberly. "They're callin' you a quitter, Davie."

David didn't answer. Both his parents had tried to shame him into torturing himself, and it hadn't worked. Now Scotty was trying. He was determined that wasn't going to work either. He knew what he was doing. When he finally threw these crutches away and walked, maybe they'd all realize he'd known all along what he was about.

"Pancakes are ready," Celia said. "Scotty, you and David get to the table." David was glad that put an end to further talk about him.

The dog lay perfectly still all through dinner, but his amber eyes watched them. Afterward David tried to tempt him with table scraps, but he pulled his head away.

"He's too sick to eat right now," Scotty said. "But he might be thirsty. He could have a fever."

Celia put a pan of water under the dog's nose. He lifted his head and lapped greedily. Then he lay back full length again.

When the dishes were washed and put away, Scotty and Celia sat at the table with the lamp between them. Scotty folded his right hand over the steel hook and

23

was ready to talk. David settled himself carefully on the floor near the dog and reached out to pat the big head. The dog pulled away, watching him warily. "All right," he murmured. He leaned against the wall to listen to the talk. Scotty was reveling in the conversation like a man satisfying a great thirst.

They began by discussing last winter's fur harvest, the prospects for this year, the kind of winter it had been, and what the coming winter might be like. "Could be bad," Scotty observed. "We've had two mild winters in a row. It's about time for a hard one."

"I hope not," Celia said. "That means more wood, food, and clothing."

"Means better fur, too," Scotty said, "and better prices."

"And harder to get around the trap line."

"And a lot harder on the dogs."

Mention of dogs brought them to dog-sled racing. They talked about the Fur Rendezvous at Anchorage and the North American and a dozen lesser races, and how the sport had grown and changed over the years. "When I was a kid," Celia said, "two or three teams would get together and race just for fun. Now it's big business, with huge cash prizes and people coming from thousands of miles away to take part and to see it."

That brought them to the people they knew and the latest news from the "outside," their term for the South Forty-eight states.

24

Celia finally said, "You know about the big oil strike, Scotty? The last time we were in Fairbanks, people were streaming in heading north of the Arctic Circle to the strike. Fairbanks is getting to be a big, modern city."

"Gold brought 'em north to begin with," Scotty said. "Then they found fur and salmon, now oil, the biggest of all. We're gonna get a lot of people up here and that'll change the country. I don't like it."

The kitchen door had been left open for ventilation, and through it David watched the last gold fade out of the sky and the distant trees rise black and solid against the night skyline. The dog slept for a time. David dozed off and when he awoke, Scotty was standing and saying apologetically, "If we don't turn in soon, it'll be morning before we know it." He offered the dog another drink, which was refused. "I can take him out to sleep in the shed with me," he said to Celia.

"Let's not move him. He seems to be comfortable."

Scotty said good night and went out to the little shed where they stored the furs in winter. A cot had been set up there for his visits. Celia went to her bedroom. David hobbled into his own room and left the door open so he could hear the dog. He undressed, got into bed, and lay listening to the sounds of the night coming through the open window. There was the occasional scrape and rattle of a dog's chain. Somewhere a fox yap-yapped excitedly. Another answered a long way off.

25

From the distant river came the unmistakeable murmur of waterfowl. A couple of the dogs barked sharply. Night breezes whispered through the big spruce at the back of the house. The tip of a limb scratched softly across the roof. David thought of the injured dog lying on the kitchen floor. Scrub wasn't much of a name to live up to, Scotty had said.

He thought of the dog's many injuries and wondered how long it would be before the animal could walk. Would he walk again when he discovered how painful it was to try? He'd learned something about pain during the months he'd been on crutches.

Yesterday, in a burst of determination, he'd set out to go to Aurora, just a mile away, to visit Nick and Jean Moore. He'd given out less than halfway there, and it had taken several slow, painful hours to hobble home on his crutches. He knew about pain and that terrible feeling of weakness. He felt discouraged, beat, sorry for himself, and now sorry for the dog whose injury was so like his own. His leg began to throb, and sleep would not come. Much later he thought he heard the dog trying to move about. He was out there in a strange place, lonesome and alone, maybe dying. Nothing should die alone. He sat up, reached for his crutches, and went quietly into the kitchen.

The moon shone through the open door and bathed the kitchen in soft light. The dog's head was up, his eyes watching David. His mouth was open, panting. David got a dish of water and put it by his head. The dog lapped it dry. He filled the pan again. The dog half-emptied the second pan, then dropped his head, and lay still.

David looked down at the dog. Then he carefully lowered himself to the floor beside him and leaned against the wall. He felt a great flood of sympathy for the unwanted, uncared-for animal. Without thinking he reached out and patted his head. The animal did not flinch or pull away. The fur between his sharp ears was silky-soft and thick. David scratched experimentally at the base of the dog's ears. "Can't sleep, huh?" he whispered. "Me either. I'll bet your leg hurts. Mine does. It always seems to hurt more at night. Guess I won't be going as far as Aurora for some time. Neither will you." The amber eyes studied the boy as the ears listened to the whispered, intimate voice. "We've got the same problem. Broken legs. You've got other injuries, but the leg's the important one." David was silent, patting the dog's head, thinking. "I guess you were in a mighty rough fight today, but you've got a lot worse one coming. Scotty says you're going to get well and he should know. But wait till you try to walk. My folks and Scotty don't know what that's like. I do."

This intimacy with a human was a new experience for Scrub. There was no threat from this boy, whose hand now offered pleasant caresses. The voice was the same quiet, sympathetic one he'd heard during the winter, when half-starved, he had been tossed sandwiches from the boy's lunch box. Scrub's tail thumped the floor feebly. With his front paws he clawed himself close and laid his big head on the boy's knee.

David smiled down at him. "I guess you've never had a friend before," he murmured. "Well, you have one now."

- 3 -

Celia Martin rose early and went into the kitchen. The sun was already high and the first heat of the day was making itself felt. She saw David and the dog in the corner. David was sound asleep, his head and shoulders propped against the log wall. The dog's head rested on his good knee. The dog lifted his head and looked at her. She bent and studied them. David's thin face was relaxed. He was smiling faintly as though enjoying some pleasant dream.

"So," she said quietly to the dog, "you've found a friend."

The dog looked at her steadily, his sharp ears forward. The voice was quiet and gentle, like the boy's. He decided to add her to his list of friends and thumped his tail on the floor to announce his decision.

"Maybe," Celia added, "you've both found a friend." David had never had a pet. All their dogs were working sled dogs. Noble, the leader, was a fine, gentle animal, but still a sled dog. It seemed to her that a boy should have a pet of his own. She touched David's shoulder. "Wake up," she said, "it's a wide, big day."

David opened his eyes and looked around. "Gee," he said sheepishly, "I went to sleep. I came out to give Scrub a drink. I only meant to sit down for a little to keep him company." He patted the dog's head, moved from under him, and carefully stood up.

Celia handed David his crutches.

"I'll get dressed." He looked down at the dog. "He looks better, don't you think, Mom?"

"He looks much better. How about you? When did you come out here?"

"Quite a while ago, I guess. I couldn't sleep. But I feel fine now."

"Then get dressed and go wake Scotty. I'll start breakfast. I've a feeling that what's-his-name, Scrub, will eat this morning."

After breakfast, Celia put the leftovers before the dog.

Scrub ate two pancakes, potatoes, and what was left of the scrambled eggs. "Nothing wrong with his insides," Scotty laughed. "Soon as that leg heals he'll be raring to go." He looked out the door. "Guess I'd better cut the wood before it gets too hot." He got the chain saw from the fur cabin and went off to the pile of logs which Fred had dragged up during the winter. Several minutes later they heard the snarl of the saw.

Celia said, "Well, will you look at that!"

Scrub had risen and, balancing on three legs, was looking out the door. He put the splinted leg on the floor, but the moment it touched he whimpered and

30

carefully lifted it again. He hobbled painfully to the open door and went outside. He made it for a few feet into the clearing and then lay down, panting. The small effort had exhausted him.

David got his crutches and followed. A hundred feet away the saw kept snarling as Scotty lobbed off the blocks. David hobbled to the log pile, found an up-ended block, and sat down. After a few minutes the dog limped up and lay at his feet. David bent and patted his head.

Scotty cut up two logs. Then he began splitting the blocks into stove wood. David was amazed at how powerfully Scotty swung the ax with one hand. By rights this was David's job when his father was gone. But on one leg he could handle neither saw nor ax. His mother had managed to split the few blocks his father had left, but the saw was too much for her.

The sun sailed high. Beads of sweat formed on Scotty's forehead. He was splitting the last block when Celia came out of the cabin and said, "That's more than enough to last until Fred comes home. Quit now, Scotty; it's getting too hot."

"You're sure it's enough? I don't want you fooling with this saw and ax."

"I'm sure, Scotty."

Scotty sat down on an upended piece of wood and wiped his face and neck with a red handkerchief. "Is kinda hot."

David kept looking at the pile of split wood. His conscience bothered him. "I should be doing that."

"For a fact you ain't worth much the way you are," Scotty said.

David was shocked at his blunt words. Even Celia looked surprised. Scotty's brown eyes were fixed on Celia, but his words were directed at David. "I did some thinking about you last night. It was too warm to sleep. Do some of my best thinking at night. Maybe I came up with something about that bad leg of yours."

Celia sat down on the end of a log, "What, Scotty?"

Scotty kept looking at her intently. "How long's it been since he broke that leg?"

"Over three months. About fifteen weeks. Why?"

"Then according to my figures Davie's right when he says it's not healed yet."

"But, the doctor said . . ."

"You told me what he said." Scotty didn't take his eyes from her face. "I'm saying he was wrong. He made a mistake. Doctors are human."

"How can that be?"

"Simple. Take this dog for example. He's got a busted leg, too. Now with him it'll take three weeks before it's well enough so he can walk on it. Dogs are roughly about six to one with people. That means Davie's should take about eighteen weeks. So he's got three more weeks before he throws these crutches away."

"I don't understand this six to one," Celia said.

"When a dog's a year old, a human's six. When a dog's two, a human's twelve."

32

"You're sure about this?"

"I had dogs more than twenty years. Even bought medical books and studied 'em so I could doctor my own animals. But it's easy to prove. Davie, you finished the eighth grade this spring. You must have studied a little science. What's the average life of a dog and a human?"

"A dog lives about ten or twelve years, a human sixty-five or seventy," David said promptly.

"There you are. Six to one. You've got about three more weeks before you throw those crutches away. You were right. It's funny the dog getting his leg broke just at this time so that when he's well enough to walk, so are you. That make sense to you, Davie?"

Scotty had presented facts David had learned in school. It was all logical. "Yes," he said.

"Remember," Scotty pointed the hook at him, "it won't be easy for either of you. It's going to be painful and hard. But this dog's going to walk again. So can you. You believe that?"

"I believe it," David said.

"Good. Now why don't you get your fish pole and meet me at the river. We'll catch a mess of trout for tonight."

David got the crutches under his arms and headed for the cabin. Scrub rose and hobbled painfully after him.

It was only about three hundred yards to the river, but it was all David and Scrub could make with several stops to rest. David sat on the bank above the clear, swift-flowing stream, the fish pole at his feet and Scrub lying beside him. There were grubs under the rocks along the water's edge that could be used for bait, but he was too tired and it was too dangerous to go down there on crutches. He lay back, an arm around Scrub's neck, and waited for Scotty.

They were both rested when Scotty finally arrived. He sat down beside Scrub, patted the dog's head, and looked about. "Great day," he observed, "bright summer sun, quiet as all get-out, a river chock-full of fish for the taking, and good company. Man couldn't hardly ask for more."

"I'd like to do some fishing," David said. "I can't do much else. But I'm afraid to crawl around among those rocks to look for bait with these crutches."

"You haven't any flies?"

"I always used grubs and sometimes a bug."

"Before I leave we'll tie you a couple of flies that'll catch fish. You'll have to do the tying. I'll supply the know-how."

"It would sure help to pass the time." David scratched at Scrub's sharp ears and thought of the talk back at the woodpile. "You really meant it that Scrub'll walk again as good as ever?"

"And run and jump. You, too, don't forget." He smiled. "You kinda like Scrub, eh?"

"He'd probably have starved a couple of times last winter if I hadn't fed him some of my lunch. Everybody was against him—other dogs, men and women, even kids. He was always sneaking around looking

34

scared and hungry. I'd like to see him get well and look fat and happy."

"He will."

"You sound so sure."

"I set the bone. It's splinted up right. Nature will do the rest. Somewhere in his dog mind he knows that, or maybe he doesn't. Anyway he instinctively helps nature out. Notice how he lies with that leg to the sun to get it warm, and how he turns his head every few minutes and tries to lick the spot where the break is? You oughta help nature along, too."

"How?" David asked.

"Pull up your pants. Let the sun get at your leg. Great healing properties in the sun's rays. Massage the muscles, get the blood pumping hard again. Exercise the muscles by moving your leg around. Help nature to get ready to start walking when Scrub does."

David thought of how Scotty had directed his mother in sewing up Scrub's rips and setting his leg, and also his knowledge of dogs' and people's ages. And now he was going to tie a couple of fishing flies. "Gee, you know a lot," David said.

"Not much when you stretch it over my years."

"When did you come north?"

"More than thirty years ago. Came from Tacoma. They called me the Tacoma Kid. I put in a year on the coast, then came up here trapping and prospecting."

"Was it different around here then?" David had asked this before and he knew about what Scotty would say, but he never tired of hearing about the north of earlier days. Scotty always added something new with each telling.

Scotty stretched out on his side, dug the steel hook into the soft earth, and began to smile as he reached back in memory more than a quarter of a century. "It was some different. Aurora wasn't here then. There wasn't another cabin in a hundred miles that I knew of. I killed my winter's meat while standing in the open door. Caribou migrated past the cabin, a hundred thousand strong, it's been estimated. They made so much racket a man couldn't sleep. They still go by, but not that many. Ducks, geese, swans, and pelicans almost blotted out the sky, it seemed like."

David rolled up his pants and let the sun warm his leg. He began massaging the flabby muscles while he listened. Scrub put his head on the boy's good knee and looked up into his face. Across the river a cow moose and calf came out of the trees. The calf lay down on the river bank. The mother waded belly-deep into the water and fed on grass growing on the bottom. A flight of ducks arrowed in and splashed to rest beyond the moose. Their excited gabbling drifted across the river. The moose fed for some minutes on the river bottom, then waded ashore. She and the calf disappeared into the timber.

"Things are different today," Scotty concluded. "But not too much right around here. There's still mighty good hunting, trapping, and fishing." That reminded him and he rose. "Son of a gun. I set here gabbing like

36

a goose, and we won't have fresh trout tonight. Then we'll both be in trouble with your mom." He picked up the fish pole. "Keep that pants leg rolled up and massage the muscles some more while I catch us a good fish feed."

Scotty found grubs under the rocks and began fishing. David continued massaging, but his leg began to ache and he quit.

It didn't take long to catch a half-dozen big trout. Scotty strung them on a forked stick, and they began the slow walk back to the cabin.

That night Scrub ate the first real meal that he didn't have to sneak, run, hide, or steal to get. Afterward he hobbled into his corner, lay down with a satisfied sigh, and went to sleep.

The next day David and Scrub made their way to the river again and stretched out side by side. David bared his leg to the sun and began gently massaging the muscles. Scrub lay on his side and tried to lick the broken leg, but the splints interfered. He gave up and went to sleep. Scotty finally arrived with the fish pole and sat down cross-legged. He had several blue-jay feathers, a crow feather, some duck down, a piece of fur that looked like it had been trimmed from Scrub when they sewed him up, and a spool of Celia's fine thread. "We're gonna make a couple of flies," he announced. "Move over here closer. You've got to supply the hands."

It took a long time and infinite patience to tie the flies to Scotty's satisfaction. David was amazed at the amount of work that went into one. Finally two were finished. Scotty held them in his palm and inspected each critically. "They don't exactly look like a professional job, and any self-respecting trout in his right mind wouldn't give 'em a second look. But I'll bet you some of 'em in this river will, because they've never seen a tied fly before." He edged up to the bank and began casting into the river. David was surprised how lifelike the fly looked skipping over the riffles. It took five or six minutes before Scotty hooked a fish. Then he caught two more in quick succession. "Come over here," he said, "I'll show you how to fly-fish."

David wiggled to the edge of the bank, and Scotty put the pole in his hands. "Now this is different from using grubs," Scotty explained. "You've got to put your mind right out there where the fly is. It's supposed to be alive. Make it act like that and keep it hopping along the water. Don't let it sink."

David cast and tried to follow Scotty's advice. The fly jumped too far, then it sank. He jerked it up, and it hopped four feet in the air. He made a dozen casts before he got the hang of making it skip. Then he worked the fly almost up to the bank, when a long dark shadow rose from the bottom and looked the fly over. David held his breath. The fly began to sink, and the fish turned away.

"Try it again," Scotty whispered excitedly. "You let the fly sink. Keep it bobbing when he comes up to inspect."

Scrub awoke and hobbled over to watch.

David tried again and again. A big shadow followed the fly right up to the bank, practically nudging the thing with its nose before turning away. Finally David hooked a fish. It headed for bottom. The pole bent. David played the fish a couple of minutes, then worked it to the top, and lifted it wriggling to the bank. Scotty shouted and clapped the boy on the back. The excitement got to Scrub, and he began to bark.

David caught two more, and Scotty said, "You've got the feel now. No sense catching more than we can eat."

The following morning Scotty announced he was going home.

"You've only been here two days," Celia said. "And you haven't seen Fred. He should be back any time."

"I got the talk outa my system for now," Scotty said. "I'll come again when Fred's home. I'll likely see you before snow flies." Before he left he inspected Scrub's splints. "Three weeks from the day we put these on, take 'em off," he said to David. "He'll be ready to walk, and so will you. Remember that. And keep exercising that leg and massaging it like you did yesterday."

"I will," David said.

Mother and son watched Scotty stride across the clearing and vanish among the trees.

That evening every dog staked out around the cabin set up a bedlam of yapping and barking that announced Fred Martin's return. He came in tall and lean and tanned, a big grin on his bony face. He was happy to be home. He kissed Celia and ruffled David's hair. Then he saw Scrub lying in the corner watching him. He scowled and said, "Hello, what've we got here?"

"A dog," David said. "He's got a broken leg."

"I can see it's a dog and not one of ours. Where'd he come from? Whose is he? What's he doing here?"

David told his father all about Scrub, how Scotty had found him, and how they had doctored him.

"One of Smiley Jackson's culls, eh?"

Celia said, "Scotty sees nothing wrong with this dog that would make him a cull."

"Well, that's Jackson for you." Fred sat down and studied the dog, scowling. "We'll have to tell Jackson his dog's here," he said finally.

"He culled him, threw him out to starve or be killed by some animal," David said. "Jackson won't nurse him back to health, Dad. He'll knock him in the head with an ax."

"I don't like the man either," Fred said, scowling. "But this is his dog and Jackson is just the type that would like to cause me some trouble if he could. We had a go-around once, and he'd like to get even."

"What kind of trouble could he cause, Dad?"

"Any kind that he thinks might pry a few dollars out of us, like accusing us of stealing his dog."

"Nobody'd believe that."

"Of course not. But Scrub is legally his, and he'd

take every advantage of it. Besides, we've got nine dogs."

"We don't have to settle this tonight," Celia said. "Let it wait until morning."

"All right. The dog's lucky Scotty found him." Fred looked at David. "How's your leg?"

"It's not well yet. Even Scotty says so."

"What's Scotty know about medicine?"

"He knows a lot."

"I'll explain later," Celia said quickly. "You must be hungry."

"I could out-eat a starving bear." He was prepared to question David further about Scotty, but he got Celia's warning look and said no more.

"Speaking of bears, what did that grizzly do to the cabin?" Celia asked as she flew about the kitchen putting a quick meal on the table.

While he ate, Fred filled them in on the grizzly raid. "What he did you wouldn't believe. All he left was the four walls and the roof. He could have torn them down if he'd wanted to. I had to completely rebuild the inside."

David heard his father but he wasn't listening. His mind was full of Scrub and of sending him back to Smiley Jackson.

David was still thinking about it when he crawled into bed later.

Next morning at breakfast, Fred announced, "We'll keep the dog until his leg's well, then I'll have to tell

Jackson he's here. What he does then will be up to him."

"Scrub will look healthy and fat by then," David said. "Jackson will want him."

"If he does, at least he won't kill him."

"I don't want Jackson to want him."

"Neither do I, Dave, but there's nothing we can do about that."

So the scrub of Aurora came to live with the Martins, if only temporarily.

- 4 -

For the first time since he was a very small pup, Scrub was not half-starved and constantly on the prowl for something to steal. Now twice a day there was all the food he could eat. He soon forgot about dodging rocks and clubs and avoiding Keno and the pack of Aurora dogs. Instead of curling up to sleep beneath a bush, in some old building, or an abandoned mine shaft, Scrub had his own blanket in a corner of the kitchen. The room was always warm, the people spoke quietly, kindly, and delicious mouth-watering odors kept his black nose twitching.

At first, he avoided the dogs staked out around the cabin. But when they paid no attention to him, he finally hobbled over to visit. Noble, the big white leader, welcomed him with much sniffing and a waving plume. In turn, the rest of the team accepted him.

Scrub was the first pet David ever had. He talked to the dog in a low, intimate voice while he scratched the thick fur of his forehead and patted the deepening chest until it boomed like a drum. "You're going to have a bigger chest than Noble in a few months," he'd say. At such times Scrub would lower his head and push it against the boy as a way of inviting more patting and scratching. "I like you, too," David said. "We make a good team."

Scrub expected to go everywhere with David and share in all his activities. The two were outside so much that Celia often had to hunt for them to come to meals. This pleased both parents, for David had been morose and listless since the accident. Now his voice would ring out across the clearing a dozen times a day, and he and Scrub would be off on some business of their own, the boy on his crutches, the dog hobbling beside, carefully holding his splinted leg above the ground.

They returned often to the river bank. It was about as far as they could hobble, taking their time, resting often. They would lie side by side in the grass and listen to the river. Often the dog's big head was on the boy's good knee. David would bare his leg to the warm sun and gently massage the weakened muscles. Scrub would doze and then try to lick the sore spots between the splints.

David spent hours fishing with the flies Scotty had tied. He became quite expert and kept the table well supplied with trout. His excitement when he hooked a fish was immense. He shouted and laughed. He played the fish expertly, finally lifting it in a clean pull to land flopping in the grass.

Scrub shared the excitement. He stood beside David

and barked encouragement. The moment the fish landed, he grabbed it and carried it to David with the air of having caught it himself. David would pat him and say, "We caught him, didn't we? I don't know what I'll do without your help." Scrub would wave his tail and lift his lips in a grin, to show that he understood they had caught the fish together.

There came a day when they made it from the cabin to the river without stopping to rest. David smiled at Scrub and said, "You're doing fine." Scrub shoved his head against David, and the boy patted his sides. "You're gaining weight. I can hardly feel your ribs. You're going to look great."

David could almost see the daily change in Scrub. As the dog filled out, the gangling, clumsy look began to disappear. His body was catching up. David was sure Jackson would want Scrub when he saw him without his splints. He tried to wipe that worry from his mind as he watched the dog grow stronger, his lean sides fill out, and the sheen come to his wolf-gray coat.

"He's beginning to look fine, don't you think, Mom?" he asked his mother one morning.

"With what he eats he should," Celia said. "That dog out-eats the three of us morning and night."

"He never had a good meal before he came here," David explained. "He's making up for lost time."

"Lost time!" His father's eyes were twinkling. "That dog's making up for time before he was born."

But no one begrudged Scrub a bite.

David was counting the days until he could walk, but each day he cared more about the changes in Scrub and himself.

A coat of tan was covering his own pale skin. His strength had improved. He was sure he could hobble to Aurora and back now. His leg muscles no longer hurt when he massaged them or when he exercised the leg. The pains he'd known at night were gone. One day he noticed that Scrub was touching his splinted leg lightly to the ground and making stepping motions with it. He tried, too, and felt only a momentary weakness and pain. From then on he put his foot down lightly, just as Scrub was doing. It was another memorable day.

The changes on the river made him most aware of the passage of time. He didn't always fish when they hobbled out there. Often he lay on the bank, with Scrub close beside him, watched the water, and let the good warm sun beat down on him. He saw the baby ducks and geese change from downy fluff-balls to small birds sprouting their first feathers. The adult birds molted, lost their primaries, and were unable to fly. They would remain earthbound until they grew new primaries for the long flight south this fall. The river level dropped, leaving a stretch of barren beach which was no hiding place for the pair of prowling foxes. The moose and calf came almost daily to the river. The calf was now sure-footed and waded into the water to feed with its mother. The lazy summer days slipped away.

The morning of the twenty-first day David said nothing to his parents. He had been unable to sleep for thinking of this day. After breakfast, his mother asked, "What are you and Scrub doing today?"

"Guess we'll go fishing."

"Good. We haven't had fish for several days. You planning anything else?"

"No." She had never asked before what he planned to do with his day. He waited, curious. She continued moving about the kitchen clearing up the breakfast dishes. "Be sure and get back for lunch," she said finally.

"I will." He hobbled outside, got the fish pole, and, with Scrub beside him, headed for the river. He was glad his parents had forgotten this was the day. He wanted to be alone with Scrub to do this his own way. If he failed, he didn't want them to see.

David lowered himself carefully in his favorite spot on the river bank and leaned the fish pole against a rock. He had no intention of fishing today. Scrub lay down beside him. The ducks and geese were busy about their business against the far shore. Their faint gabbling was the only sound this still morning. A small breeze barely stirred the leaves. He guessed the moose and her calf wouldn't come until later in the day. But David was not interested in the ducks and geese or thinking about the moose. Finally he patted Scrub's big head and said, "Scotty told us this would be the day. I guess there's no use waiting any longer. You first."

David began loosening the splints. His fingers trembled. "It's going to hurt like sixty," he said. "But here goes." He carefully unwound the binding and took the splints off. "There you are. You can try it any time." He watched the dog intently.

Scrub smelled his leg and licked the broken spot. He rose, still on three legs, and took a couple of hobbling steps. Then he seemed to realize the bandages and splints were gone. He put the paw on the ground and immediately lifted it. For a moment he balanced there, then carefully lowered the foot again. He hobbled off a few feet, then turned and came back and lay down. That small exertion seemed to have exhausted him.

David knew what the dog was going through. Scotty had been wrong. The leg was not healed. Scrub was aware of this and quit just as David had been forced to do.

But soon the dog was up again. He limped a few steps and stopped. But he didn't lie down. He began walking again and limped a circle around David, head down, ears flattened to his head. He wandered off and returned. David could see, or he imagined, the dog was putting more weight on the leg. The limp seemed a little less pronounced. Scrub walked farther between stops.

David's fists were clenched. What had Scotty said? "He'll endure pain. He does what nature tells him he has to do to walk again." Scotty had been right! Scrub's leg was healed! The dog was proving it with every step. David called Scrub to him and patted his head. He held the big head between his hands and shook him lovingly. "You made it! You made it!" Scrub wagged his tail and lifted his lips in a grin. David drew a deep breath. "Scotty said when you walked I could. Well, here goes!"

David got carefully to his feet and balanced on the crutches. His palms were wet. He was shaking and for a moment could not stop. This was the day he'd waited so long for, and now he was afraid. He straightened his leg gingerly, put his foot flat on the ground, and bore down with weight. He dropped the crutches and stood. Pain was a knife that made him lift the foot as Scrub had done. Maybe if he tried to walk. He got off three quick steps, then the weakened leg folded. He sprawled full-length, wrenching the muscles of the leg as he fell. David rolled over and sat up holding the leg with both hands. He wasn't crying. But he couldn't stop tears from squeezing between his shut lids. Then he felt Scrub's warm tongue licking his cheek. David put his arms around the furry neck and held the dog close until the worst of the pain had passed. Then he got up and tried again.

He balanced on the good leg and brought his weight down carefully on the bad one. The pain was no worse. He knew then that his task, too, was to endure the pain. David managed a grin at Scrub and said, "You're not the only one can walk." He picked out a big rock as target a few steps away—and made it. Next he limped a circle around the rock, close enough so that he could grab it if he started to fall. He didn't.

David leaned against the rock and rested a couple of minutes. Then he picked up the crutches, limped to the edge of the bank, and hurled them into the river. "Come on," he said triumphantly to Scrub, "let's go home."

It was not the proud, heads-up, joyous return David had visualized. It was slow and painful, and they had to stop several times to rest. The dog made better time than the boy. But he slowed his pace and they traveled together. They went through the trees and across the clearing to the cabin. When David stepped through the door, his mother and father were in the kitchen. He had planned to say something exciting and dramatic, but all he could think of was the great distance they'd come, and he said, "We made it. We both made it."

"You sure did." His father gripped his arm. "You sure did, son." Then he turned his head quickly away.

David noticed there was dirt on both his father's and mother's shoes. Fresh grass stems were caught in the eyelets, as would happen if you ran through grass. "You followed us," David said. "You saw."

"Oh, David, we had to know," his mother said. "We were sure you and Scrub would try, and we guessed you wanted to be alone." She put her arms around him and began to cry.

- 5 -

Fred Martin thoughtfully rubbed his jaw with a big hand as he looked at Scrub. "Guess it's time to tell Smiley Jackson we've got his scrub dog."

Scrub lifted his head from the corner in the kitchen and thumped his tail on the floor.

David said quickly, "He still limps a little, Dad. Can't we wait a few days?"

"Waiting will only make it harder."

"If Jackson sees him now he'll want him," David protested.

"Very likely. Now even Jackson can see the kind of dog he's going to become. At least you don't have to worry about him knocking Scrub in the head. He'll be too valuable."

"Smiley Jackson's no good," David said harshly. "Why do we have to tell him at all? He must think Scrub's dead since he hasn't showed up around Aurora these past weeks. And he would be if Scotty hadn't found him. Why can't we keep him and say nothing? Jackson hardly ever comes this way. He threw Scrub out to die and made him into a stray. We earned him."

"Suppose we did keep Scrub and Jackson doesn't see him, which is highly unlikely. Eventually somebody else will recognize the dog. The word would get back to Jackson. He's the ratty kind who'd make us all the trouble he could. Jackson and I aren't exactly friends," Fred said.

"Nobody's his friend," David said.

His mother's dark head turned toward her son. "There's more to it than that. Your father told you he had trouble with Jackson. Well, it was a knockdown fight and your father gave him a good beating," she said with satisfaction. "Jackson called him a squaw man because I'm an Indian."

"Celia!" Fred said sharply.

"David's old enough now," Celia said. "He's got to know."

"Why didn't you tell me before?"

"You had to go to school in Aurora. We didn't want you to feel different from the other children until you were old enough to understand the situation."

"I knew Dad had a fight," David said. "I didn't know it was with Jackson. I was only about six. I didn't pay much attention to what went on with the older people." He looked at his father, "Did you give Jackson that scar?"

"He had that when we came, got it in a fight with someone else. But you see what we're up against. Jackson never forgets. He'll be trying to get back at me for that beating till the day he dies."

52

"I guess so," David said.

"If you want a pet, what's wrong with Noble?" Fred asked quietly.

Noble was smart and gentle. But Scrub and David had formed a bond that was stronger than dog and master. They were equals. But he couldn't explain this to his father. He said lamely, "It wouldn't be the same, Dad."

Fred ruffled his hair, "I think I understand. I'm sorry there's no other way. With most anybody else we could have worked out something—not with Jackson." He slipped into his coat and went off across the clearing.

David wandered about the kitchen, watching the clock and the trail that led to Aurora. Scrub lay in his corner and wagged his tail whenever the boy glanced his way.

Celia was baking bread. She thumped the big roll of dough on the breadboard and kneaded it angrily.

An hour dragged by. The bread went into baking pans, then finally into the oven. Celia began cleaning up. David sat down beside Scrub and put his arm around the dog's neck. "Dad ought to be back by now, hadn't he?"

"How should I know?" she snapped. Then she turned and said gently, "Don't watch the clock, David. Minute-counting makes it longer. He's only been gone an hour and fifteen minutes."

Scrub put his head on David's knee. The boy scratched his ears and patted him between the eyes.

The first loaves came out of the oven and a delicious aroma spread through the room. Celia sliced off the hot heel, spread it with jam, and handed it to David. It was one of his favorite treats, but he couldn't eat now. He tore it into small pieces and fed them to Scrub.

"You think Jackson will come back with Dad?"

"He might. It wouldn't surprise me if he wanted us to keep his dog until he's completely well."

Noble began to bark. David scrambled to his feet as his father came through the door. He was alone.

"What took so long?" Celia asked.

"He was gone. I had to wait for him." Fred shook his head angrily. "I always knew he didn't have the brains of a mosquito, but I didn't realize how dumb he really is. I told him we had his dog and what had happened to him. What do you suppose he said?" He mimicked Smiley Jackson's nasal twang. "Well, I wondered what'd happened to 'im. Ain't seen 'im around in three, four weeks. Figured a bear might'a got 'im or somethin'. So he's got a busted leg, huh, and you want me to take 'im back. Not a chance. I culled 'im last winter. He ain't worth a bullet to kill 'im. He's your responsibility now. You get rid of 'im. Don't come cryin' t' me."

"Did you tell him Scrubby was practically well now?" Celia asked.

"I said he was able to walk again. I couldn't have changed his mind no matter what I'd said. He had decided Scrub was no good months ago. Jackson thinks he's the great authority."

54

"Did you tell him the kind of dog Scrub's becoming?" David asked.

His father's dark eyes twinkled. "Why, you know I couldn't do that. It would be my opinion against his expert judgment."

Scrub felt the excitement. He rose and stood beside David. Fred scratched the dog's head. "I guess you've got a home at last, fella."

Scrub waved his tail and barked.

Fred wrinkled his nose. "That fresh bread sure smells good."

David was suddenly hungry. "I could eat some, Mom."

Celia cut a slice, spread it with jam, and handed it to him. Scrub watched the bread and licked his lips. "You still hungry, Scrubby?" Celia asked as she sliced off a thick piece, spread it liberally with jam, and held it out. Scrub took it daintily in his teeth and followed David outside.

"Hey!" Fred said, "that's good bread."

"So?" Celia asked archly.

"So how about me? I'm as good as any dog here."

Within a couple of days, neither boy nor dog were limping. In a week, they were racing pell-mell through the woods and along the river bank. Except in the company of his father David had never explored the country more than a mile or two from home. Now, with Scrub, he was anxious to go out alone.

"I don't know," Celia said doubtfully. "What do you think, Fred?"

"Why not?" his father answered promptly. "He's got his own light rifle, and he's a pretty fair shot. The rifle will handle any game he's likely to meet."

"What about grizzlies, black bears, and moose?" Celia asked.

"There are no grizzlies around here. Forty or fifty miles away, sure. But not here. There's a few blacks, but they'll be hightailing it out to get away from Scrub. Moose aren't ugly this time of year, but he can give them a wide berth. He's got a compass and knows how to use it. If he should become lost, Scrub could lead the way home. It'll toughen him up so he can help run the trap line this winter."

"Well, all right." Celia patted Scrub's big head. "You take good care of David, Scrubby."

Carrying the rifle, and his lunch in a small knapsack, David, with Scrub beside him, headed out morning after morning. The two were gone most of the day. They followed small streams to where they emptied into rivers or tumbled into deep, quiet lakes that nestled in the cups of the mountains. They hiked over rolling, bread-loaf hills that were crowned with thick stands of timber. They found streams so small that they could easily step across them. Then again their way might be barred by a brawling river that charged in white-frothed fury between rock-jawed banks. One day they lay on the shore of a lake and watched young ducks and geese trying out their new wings while skimming uncertainly across the still surface.

They dropped into miniature valleys where beaver

56

had dammed small streams to form lakes that teemed with fish and waterfowl. David lay flat on his back in the long grass of a meadow with Scrub beside him, while they shared lunch and listened to the varied sounds of the earth. They heard the distant call of a loon, the chatter of a jay. A pair of crows talked companionably in the thicket. A short distance off, a muskrat sat on top of his house, which had been built at the edge of a pond. A flight of ducks arrowed in, wind whistling in their set wings. They splashed noisily to rest in the pond. Leaves rustled in the warm breeze. And beside his ear, David heard the faint whisper of grass stems springing erect again where his careless feet had tramped them flat.

The days were long and warm and pleasant. They ate lunch in the shade of a rock, on a stream bank, beside a lake, or on top of a hill, with the earth spread out below them. They drank from crystal-clear streams. Once David went swimming while Scrub stood on the bank and barked with worry.

Scrub continued to gain weight but now it was ropes of muscle that spanned his shoulders and the breadth of his chest. The addition of muscle gave him a sturdy look. The youthful awkwardness was gone. He had entered into young doghood and was becoming especially quick and nimble. He could run with amazing speed.

Fred said, "He's going to be quite a dog; in fact he is. I'd guess at full maturity he'll go close to a hundred pounds."

One morning the cabin roof was white with frost.

The faint breeze had a cutting edge. Leaves browned and fell whispering into the grass. The grass that had grown with such lusty vigor died overnight. Fall was suddenly upon them. The waterways emptied of ducks and geese. The great migrations formed into huge V's and went winging south. The birds' farewell calls filtered down through gathering cloud masses. The silence of approaching winter closed over the earth. The sun lost its heat. Ice formed along the banks of the river where David and Scrub had fished.

Scotty did not make it back for a visit before first snow fell.

With a good snowfall covering the ground, David and Fred started out to set their more than five hundred traps. David had never gone on the trap line before. He rode in the sled's basket. Scrub trotted alongside, tail curled over his back, grinning from ear to ear. They had an eighty-mile circle to cover. There were four cabins at regular intervals where they could spend the night. Scotty's made a fifth cabin a mile off their trap line. It was slow work setting the traps the first time. It was even slower because Fred showed David how to make each set. Then he had the boy duplicate it.

"When you're ready," Fred explained, "we'll lengthen the line, split it up, and both work it. But first you've got to know everything I do." He asked once if David wanted to try handling the team.

David said, "No."

His father didn't ask again.

The first night Fred staked Scrub out with the other dogs. The moment David entered the cabin and closed the door, Scrub began to howl. He kept it up until David went out and brought him in. "Guess I made a mistake," Fred grinned. "He's a house dog and knows it."

Scrub ate in the cabin with them. That night he slept on the dirt floor beside David's bunk. From then on that was how it was.

The third morning, they were hitching up the team while Scrub sat on his tail a few feet off, watching interestedly. David said, "Dad, let's put Scrub in and see what he does."

"Why not? He's certainly big and strong enough. Jack's getting a little old. We'll take him out and let him follow along."

They buckled Scrub into the harness between Spot and Ginger. Scrub kept turning around trying to go back to David in the sled, but the harness stopped him. At Fred's shout, the team was off, dragging Scrub with it. He hung back, fighting to get free. He growled and snarled. Ginger promptly nipped him as a warning. Scrub whirled to tear into Ginger, and Spot took him from the other side. He was caught between the two dogs. The harness kept him from backing off to get them in front of him. The rest of the team kept pulling. Scrub was being hit from behind, in front, and dragged, too. He was forced to turn and run. After a couple of miles of alternately trying to whirl and fight his tormentors and being dragged, he finally began to run with the team. By the end of the day he was having little trouble.

"He's doing fine," Fred said. "You want to leave him in?"

"Might as well. I think he's beginning to enjoy it."

Scrub stayed in harness, and he did seem to enjoy using his young strength. He was sharp and observing. He ran with his big head up, amber eyes searching out ahead, tongue lolling out in a grin. He could see Noble, and he observed how the lead dog skirted a dangerous patch of rotting ice that Scrub felt bend beneath their weight when they came close. Noble turned out to avoid snow-covered rocks or stumps that could smash the sled. He set the pace and kept the team strung out. The team followed whatever Noble did. When the man spoke, it was always to Noble.

The fifth night, they made Scotty's cabin. The following night they would be home.

"I see you got rid of the crutches," Scotty said to David.

"Just like you said," David smiled. "And look at Scrub."

Scotty examined Scrub and patted his head. "You turned out about like I figured you would, friend. Does Smiley Jackson know where you are?"

"He knows," David said. "Dad told him, but he wouldn't even come to see Scrub. He told Dad to get rid of him."

60

"That's Smiley Jackson for you," Scotty said.

Scrub had crowded into the cabin with them and David said, "Do you mind, Scotty? He always comes in. He sleeps beside my bunk."

Scotty shrugged. "I had my whole team in the cabin sometimes." He picked up a frying pan. "How's bacon pancakes strike you fellows?"

"Fine," David and Fred chorused.

Scotty looked at Scrub. "How about you, friend?"

Scrub waved his tail and lifted his lips in a grin.

"Bacon pancakes it is," Scotty said.

They left Scotty's before daylight next morning, and Scrub was still in harness, with Jack trotting alongside. They made good time and by late afternoon were within a couple of miles of home, when they rounded a thicket and found Smiley Jackson resting his young team in the trail.

Black Keno was the leader. The team was composed of some of the young dogs that had made up the pack which had harassed Scrub all winter.

Noble turned out to go around, and Smiley yelled, "Hey, wait a minute!"

Fred stopped and looked at Jackson.

Jackson left his team and walked straight up to Scrub. David held his breath.

"That's my dog," Jackson said accusingly.

"It's the cull you kicked out to starve," Fred said. "The one with the broken leg, remember?"

"Seems like it got all right. You workin' him now?"

61

"Just giving him a little exercise."

"He's lookin' pretty good. Bigger'n any dog I got, even Keno."

"He wouldn't be alive if we hadn't cared for him."

Jackson ignored the thrust. "Can't never tell f'r sure how a pup'll turn out. I don't get surprised often. But this one fooled me." He returned to his team, stepped on the runners, and yelled. The whip snaked out and exploded like a rifle. He tore off in a shower of snow, the whip cracking at regular intervals.

"Any time you want lessons on how to ruin a team, watch Smiley Jackson," Fred said disgustedly.

"He was surprised about Scrub," David said.

"He certainly was. Noble, let's go home."

Winter's early dark closed down. The sled was unloaded and turned on its side against the cabin wall. The dogs were staked out and fed. During dinner Fred filled Celia in on everything that had happened during their six days on the trail.

"We put Scrub in harness, Mom," David said. "You should have seen him. He caught on real fast."

"Naturally," Celia said. "Scrubby's a smart dog."

"He had a couple of good teachers, too—Spot and Ginger." Fred smiled.

They finished dinner, and David helped his mother clear the table and wash the dishes. Fred settled in a chair to read the Anchorage paper. Outside, Noble barked sharply, and other dogs chimed in. Fred muttered, "Probably a rabbit."

Then a knock came at the door.

Fred opened the door, and Smiley Jackson walked in. He scrubbed a hand across his perpetually grinning lips. He'd been drinking, but he was not drunk. He carried a short length of chain. His beady eyes darted about the room and spotted Scrub. "I come f'r my dog."

Fred barred his way. "You don't just walk in here and start taking things," he said coldly.

"Do, when it's my dog."

"Who says he's your dog?"

"Out'a my bitch, Goldie. That makes him my dog."

"You culled him, kicked him out to starve or be killed."

"Still my dog, all square and legal." Smiley Jackson started forward again, and Fred put out a big hand and stopped him.

"When I told you he was here, you couldn't be bothered to look at him. You said he never was any good, and with a broken leg he'd be worse. He's still the same dog."

"You didn't say how good he looked," Jackson said.

"He didn't look good then."

"He does now."

"You forfeited all rights to this dog when you threw him out."

"Show me that in writin'," Jackson challenged. "Everybody in Aurora knows he's mine."

Celia said quickly, "Mr. Jackson, how much do you want for the dog? We'll buy him. He's David's pet now."

"You don't say!" Jackson's weasel eyes narrowed at the thought of money. "That dog's got the makin's of a valuable animal. With his size and strength he'll be a fine sled dog."

"Maybe," Fred said. "Quit building it up. Set a price."

Jackson scratched his whiskery jaw. "Tell you what. Gimme five hundred dollars, and your kid's got a pet."

"Come off it!" Fred said angrily. "That's the price of a well-trained sled dog."

"Which he'll be when I get through with 'im."

"Five hundred!" Celia said, shocked.

"Cash money." Jackson held out a grimy paw.

"You're crazy," Fred said.

"Sure I am," Jackson said. "Five hundred or I take 'im."

The moment David saw Jackson in the open door, shock rolled through him and he'd gone immediately to Scrub. Now he squatted on the floor, his arm around the dog while the argument broke over him. Scrub was sitting up, his body tense at the sounds of angry voices. Every time he heard Jackson's nasal twang, the edges of his lips curled.

"The price for the average trained sled dog is three hundred," Fred said. "That's what I'll give you."

"He won't be average," Jackson said. "I'll take my dog."

"What are you going to do with him?" David asked fearfully.

"None of your business, boy."

64

"Dad," David said, "you're not going to let him have Scrub?"

"I'll split the difference with you," Fred said. "Four hundred. You'll be getting more than a trained-dog price for one that's green and untried."

Jackson shook his head. "I got a feelin' he ain't so green an' untried as you're sayin'."

Celia said, very businesslike, "We'll give you five hundred, Mr. Jackson. Now then, we cared for Scrub, nursed him back to health, and have fed him for months. We'll subtract that from the five hundred and pay you the difference."

"I didn't give you authority to do a thing to that dog," Jackson said. "You did that on your own, so you're out whatever it cost you. But I'll tell you what I will do. I'll make it four fifty. That's your last chance."

"All right," Fred agreed. "But you'll have to wait until I can sell some fur."

Jackson shook his head. "Four fifty. Cash in hand now. Tonight."

"I don't have the cash, but you'll get your money."

"No cash," Jackson said, "no dog."

"You had no intention of selling him to us," Celia said angrily.

Jackson's lips pulled into a gargoyle smile. He said to Fred, "Tell your kid to get away from my property."

David saw his father's big fists knot. Muscles bunched along his lean jaws. Then he said quietly, "Dave, get away from Scrub."

"No!" David said fiercely. "Not after all we've done, after he's lived with us. He can't."

His father repeated, "Get away, Dave."

"I won't. Scrub's not going back with him. Mom!"

She shook her head. "Don't make it harder than it is."

"Mom, we can't. It's not right."

Her voice was sharp: "Do as your father says. Now!"

David looked into her snapping black eyes, at his father's stormy face. There was no help anywhere. He took his arm slowly from Scrub's neck and stood up. He didn't want to watch Jackson cross the room with that grin on his face and snap the chain around Scrub's neck. But he couldn't take his eyes away.

"Come on," Jackson jerked on the chain.

Scrub turned his head and looked at David.

Jackson yanked brutally and Scrub lifted his lips. "So," Jackson said, "I gotta show you who's boss."

"Don't yank that chain again," Fred said sharply.

"I'll handle 'im my way."

"Not in this house. Now get hold of that chain and take him out right," Fred's voice was commanding. "And do it now!"

Jackson looked at the big man and his smirk disappeared. He took hold of the chain close to Scrub's neck, literally lifted the dog to his feet, and pulled him toward the door. Scrub braced his feet and twisted his head around, searching for David. He began to whine.

David started forward and was stopped by his father's sharp "Hold it, Dave." Then Fred blocked

66

Jackson's way a last time. His eyes hit Jackson with so driving a look that the man could not meet it. "If you ever come out here again for any reason at all, I'll stomp you out of sight in the ground. You remember that. Now get out."

"No reason to come back. I got my property." Jackson went out, dragging the struggling, whining Scrub.

Fred closed the door and looked at his son. "I'm sorry, Dave. The law was on his side. And it can be coldblooded and brutal."

David's throat was so full he couldn't speak. The room blurred. He didn't look at his mother. She was crying. He turned blindly into his room and slammed the door. A part of him had been cruelly torn away this night. Nothing would ever be the same again.

- 6 -

Things were not the same for Scrub at Smiley Jackson's. He wasn't allowed in the cabin. He was staked to a ten-foot chain like the rest of Jackson's dogs. His only shelter from snow and storm would be his own heavy, wolf-gray coat and the hole he'd dig in the snow. He dug the hole the first night, curled up with his nose tucked into the thick fur of his stomach, and let the snow drift over him. Next morning, when Jackson appeared to hitch up the team for a practice run, Scrub knew what was coming. All the dogs were up and waiting expectantly.

Jackson took Keno first. He passed Scrub as he led the first dog to the sled. When the two dogs came opposite, Keno stopped. Here was a dog he had not yet disciplined. He had fought every dog in the team to prove his leadership. He would establish his mastery over this one. Keno growled and showed his teeth.

Scrub remembered Keno. Now he was not the half-starved, clumsy pup of last summer. He stood several inches above Keno at the shoulders. He was broader, deeper of chest. The clumsiness of puppy days had disappeared. Maturity, food, and loving care had added weight and muscle. He waited, head down, amber eyes looking obliquely up as he measured Keno.

Jackson knew Keno must assert his mastery over Scrub. There was no better time than the present. Scrub was still chained and had only a few feet to move. That would make Keno's job easier. Jackson unsnapped the leader's chain and said, "Take 'im, Keno!"

Keno lunged at Scrub as he had last summer, as he had at every dog in the team that he'd fought. His sudden attacks had proved successful in the past. But when his teeth snapped together, Scrub was not there. He had dodged Keno's lunge, and as the black dog flashed by, Scrub struck with lightning speed and ripped Keno's shoulder to the bone. Keno whirled, and the two came together, reared on hind legs, fangs slashing. As before, Keno drove for the throat, only to be met by Scrub's fangs. Scrub's greater weight and strength drove him slipping backward through the snow until the chain jerked him up short.

Keno did not rush in again. He had felt the strength and quickness of the wolf-gray dog. He became cautious and circled just beyond reach of the chain, looking for an opening, snarling horribly. At the end of his chain Scrub turned with him, head down, lips lifted, watching and waiting.

Jackson said impatiently, "Go on, Keno, get it over with. Take 'im! Take 'im!"

Thus encouraged, Keno leaped to the attack again.

Scrub shot in under the black dog, caught a front leg in his jaws, and jerked Keno forward where he could get at him. In a flash, he flipped Keno on his back and straddled his chest. His big teeth were at Keno's unprotected throat. Keno, knowing death was but the snap of Scrub's teeth away, relaxed and lay perfectly still. It was a dog's way of admitting defeat and asking for mercy. For a moment Scrub stood over him, a growl rumbling in his throat, every tooth in his head showing. Then he backed off. Keno rolled over, got painfully to his feet, and limped away. Scrub stood there, head high, glaring about at the other dogs. Challenge was in every inch of him.

Jackson caught Keno and chained him again. With that ripped shoulder and injured leg, he couldn't be used for at least a week. He stood looking at Scrub angrily, surprised at how easily he'd beaten Keno. Scrub had destroyed Keno as a leader. Now Jackson needed another. He studied the wolf-gray dog, making up his mind. Then he unfastened the chain and led him to Keno's lead spot and buckled him into the harness.

"You're the toughest, all right," he growled. "You'd better get to be the smartest in a hurry or you'll wind up with a bullet between the eyes."

Scrub had learned to follow Noble and the team. He had not learned to lead. But when Jackson popped the whip over his back and yelled, he knew exactly where he was going. All night he'd thought of but one thing, the boy and cabin in the clearing. Now that he was not chained and there was no one in front of him, he headed back as fast as his legs would carry him. Jackson's shouts and curses, the cracking of the whip, meant nothing.

Jackson finally dumped the sled on its side. This acted as a powerful brake that stopped the team. Jackson rushed at Scrub and kicked him. Then he began using the whip. His insane temper was loose and his one desire was to punish. Scrub could not run away or dodge the lash. He could only crouch and take the beating. Jackson was an expert with the whip, and every swing of his arm cut or raised welts on the cringing dog. When Jackson finally stopped, he'd administered as thorough a beating as he'd ever given an animal. He righted the sled and yelled. Scrub got painfully to his feet and did as he was told. But his ribs ached and his muscles were sore. He burned from a dozen welts and lash cuts. For a time he barely kept ahead of the team. The worst of the pain finally wore off, and he was able to run again.

Scrub was not through making mistakes that first day. They hit a stump and almost wrecked the sled. He didn't turn out far enough, and the sled hit a rock and flipped over. Jackson held his temper until they headed home. They were traveling in the direction of the boy and the cabin in the clearing. The closer they got the more excited Scrub became. At last he was returning. He was running faster and faster, showing Jackson a speed he'd never found in a lead dog before. But when Jackson tried to turn him toward Aurora and his own cabin, Scrub ran straight on. Once more Jackson flipped the sled on its side to stop them. Again he gave Scrub a sound beating.

When they arrived at the cabin and Jackson had the team staked out, he stood looking at Scrub. The dog was lying down, panting. He was near exhaustion and was hurting from the lash burns.

"Maybe you'll make a lead dog," Jackson said darkly. "Maybe not. But one thing I know. I'll beat that Martin kid out'a your head or I'll kill you."

In the weeks that followed, Scrub became a strong lead dog. Jackson was a brutal taskmaster. He had no feeling for a dog. He let Scrub control the team, but he controlled Scrub. This he did by liberal use of his feet and the lash. There was no praise when the dog did well. He simply did not feel the lash then.

Scrub lost weight. He was fed but once a day now, and never as much as he wanted. But he became tough and hard. He was always on the chain except when Jackson put him in harness. Keno returned to the team and added strength and speed. He and Scrub had no more trouble. They were a young team. The toughening and discipline required for racing took long hours of hard work. At first Jackson ran the sled empty. Then, as their strength increased, he began piling on wood for weight. He lengthened the run and shortened the rest stops. Day after day he brought them staggering back to Aurora.

Scrub no longer headed for the Martins' cabin when they drew near. But Jackson had not beat the memory

72

of the boy out of his mind. Each time they approached the turnoff, Scrub searched hopefully for a sight of David. Night after night he howled his loneliness and longing. This brought Jackson with the whip, and finally Scrub's howling stopped. But his mourning was in no way lessened. He curled up, nose tucked into the warm fur of his stomach, and brooded silently. He waited and watched. There would come a time when the man grew careless.

This was the most promising team Jackson had ever owned. He bragged about it, until finally the owner of the trading post timed him with a stopwatch. He made it in a fraction less than ten minutes over a two-mile course. That was almost championship time, and the team was still green. Everyone was impressed. It would be an honor for Aurora to have a championship team —even with a musher like Smiley Jackson. So they watched and hoped, but doubted. The success of any team depends in great measure upon the leader. Everyone knew the history of the scrub of Aurora.

David missed Scrub more than anything in his life. He wandered about the cabin, looked out the window at the snow, and said, "Scrub won't have a house. He has to sleep in the snow."

"Scrub will be all right," Celia said. "He has a good thick coat. Jackson's dogs always sleep out. It hasn't hurt them."

"Ours don't, except when Dad's on the trail."

73

"Your father's not Smiley Jackson."

"I could sneak up through the brush and look at him."

"You keep away from Jackson's," Celia warned.

"He wouldn't know I was there. I'd stay hidden in the brush."

"One of the dogs might smell you, or see you, and start barking. Next thing Jackson would be out."

"What could he do? I'd just be looking."

"If he happened to be drunk, there's no telling. You know about his temper."

"Going up there is only torturing yourself," Fred said.

"I'd like to know how he is, Dad."

"I can tell you one thing. I was coming over that hill between here and Aurora yesterday, and I saw Jackson coming back from a practice run. Scrub is his new lead dog."

"Lead dog!" David said excitedly. "How was he doing?"

"It was rough. But then he's new at it. I've a hunch he'll be all right. So you see, being the leader, Jackson's going to treat him better than the rest."

"That's not saying much."

"At least it's something." Fred added after a moment, "I'm heading out on the trap line tomorrow morning. You'd better come along if you're going to learn how this is done, so we can lengthen the line next year. Besides, moping around the house won't help. You need something to do to forget."

74

The only time David had ever been on the trap line was when he'd helped his father set out the traps earlier. This was his first time out when they were actually taking fur. There was much to learn. Traps had to be set and reset. Occasionally they had to move traps to new locations. Baits were cleverly stolen and had to be replenished. At several, the brush and twig camouflage that hid the traps had been ripped away and had to be rebuilt. Each night they spent carefully skinning out the fur that had been taken that day. This work should have made David too tired to think of Scrub. But he remembered the big dog at odd moments. Often, on the trail, Noble glanced back, tongue lolling out, lips lifted in a grin, the way Scrub used to do. When Ginger nipped Jack, who was in harness in Scrub's place, David had to smile, remembering Scrub's first experience as a sled dog. Every night when they staked out the team, he thought of the howl Scrub put up to come into the cabin with him.

He awoke several times each night and thoughtlessly trailed a hand over the side of the bunk. When he found no sharp ears and cold nose, aching loss overwhelmed him.

The fifth night, they made Scotty's. He ran an eye over the team and asked, "Where's my friend? Where's Scrub?"

David didn't answer. Fred said, "Jackson saw him. We had quite an argument later. But Jackson took the dog."

Scotty nodded. "That figured to happen if Jackson

75

laid eyes on him." He was about to say more, then glanced at David's face, and said nothing. They unhitched and staked out the team in silence.

In the warm cabin, Scotty asked, "Well, what's for supper? Anybody for bacon pancakes?"

David said nothing. Scotty had jokingly asked Scrub that very question on their last trip. Scrub had pounded his tail on the floor and grinned from ear to ear.

Fred said, "That'll be fine."

For the first time in the years he'd known Scotty, David wished they'd had something else to eat that night.

When they arrived home, Celia said, "My, am I glad you're back! Do you know how long a week is alone in winter? I almost got cabin fever. I wish I could go along."

"I don't like being gone so much," Fred said. "But that's trapping." He rubbed his jaw thoughtfully. "Dave's doing fine keeping the cabins cleaned up, cooking, and he's learning to set traps and skin."

"What are you getting at?" Celia asked.

"There's more to trapping. Learning to be alone is a big part of it."

"So?"

"Let him start learning."

"That's in the future."

"Not so far," Fred said. "He'll be old enough to run a line alone by next year."

"Do you really think so?"

"Other boys have done it. He's got everything here

76

to do with," Fred pointed out. "The trick of being alone is learning to keep yourself busy at something. It's not as easy as it sounds. You have to learn by yourself. Right here is a good place to start. The two of you can alternate. You can go on the line with me one week, Dave the next. That way you won't be alone so much."

"I don't know." Celia looked at David. "Would you mind being alone a week?"

"I think it's a great idea," David said. "You go next time. I'll make out fine."

"You've never been alone," Celia said uncertainly.

"It's time he started," Fred said. "Let him grow up."

"Don't worry," David said. "I'll find plenty to do."

"Well, all right. I went along before he was born. Remember?"

Fred smiled. "Be a little like old times."

It was still dark when they left the second morning. Celia, bundled in her parka and with a robe wrapped about her, rode in the basket. Her face looked small and childishly excited framed in the parka hood. She waved and called, "You be careful. Hear?"

Fred said, "See you in a week, Dave. Take care." He shouted at Noble. The team lunged into the harnesses, and they were off.

David cleaned up the breakfast dishes and made his bed. He spent an hour splitting wood and filled the wood box. The snow was soft, the air crisp and sharp. A brittle sun made ice diamonds on every bush and tree. He decided to go for a hike and got into his parka. It was easy traveling, and he went out along the frozen river where Scrub and he had spent much time and learned to walk. A snowshoe rabbit watched him from the edge of the brush, then turned, and quickly disappeared. A flock of ptarmigans exploded out of the snow and zoomed across the frozen river. Moose, rabbit, and fox tracks laced the smooth snow blanket covering the ice. Then he remembered his father had seen Scrub with Jackson's team near that hill between the cabin and Aurora. He headed for the hill.

The hill was several hundred feet high and barren of brush and trees. From the top he looked over the country, dotted with brush patches and a scattering of timber all heavily laden with snow. At the bottom of the hill a single set of sled tracks marred the smooth whiteness. If those were Jackson's and he came this way again, he'd be close enough to see Scrub from here. He sat on a rock to wait.

The cold crept through his heavy clothing and chilled him. From time to time he walked around the rock, stomped his feet, and swung his arms to keep warm. The heatless sun fell down the sky. Long shadows lay across the snow. David was about to give up and return home when, far in the distance, a dog team moved on the white expanse. It crept steadily forward. The faint crack of the driver's whip rode the silence. Smiley Jackson's nasal voice floated up to him.

David squatted behind the rock and watched. The struggling team drew near. The sled was loaded with great chunks of wood to make the dogs work harder. He recognized Scrub in the lead. His big head was down. He was digging in with all his strength, as was every other dog. Jackson was shouting. The whip snaked out again and again and popped over the dogs' straining backs. David wanted to rush down, snatch the whip from Jackson, and use it on the man. The team passed beneath him, rounded the base of the hill, and was out of sight.

David was back at the same spot the next day. He saw the team come into sight, struggling as before. The whip popped, and Jackson shouted. They stopped at the foot of the hill to untangle one of the dogs. David studied Scrub. He looked tired and unhappy. His sharp ears were down. His mouth was open, panting. Even at this distance David could see Scrub had lost weight. A minute later the tangled dog was freed. Jackson cracked the whip and shouted. The team struggled on and disappeared.

David thought about Scrub the rest of the day. That night, after he'd eaten, he put all the scraps in a sack, put on his parka, and went off through the starlit night toward Aurora.

Jackson's cabin was about a quarter of a mile from Aurora. David stole through protective brush to within a hundred feet. He crouched behind a bush and studied the cabin. There was a light in the window. Smoke drifted from the chimney.

He watched and listened for several minutes, but there was no sound from the cabin. The dogs were dark humps curled up in the snow. David tried to figure which one was Scrub, but they all looked alike. He stole forward silently, hoping they would not start up a racket.

The first dog raised his head and looked at him, then curled up again. The second was black. He guessed that would be Keno. He passed the next and the next. His carefully placed feet scarcely whispered in the snow. Each dog looked up at David. Not one barked.

The next head to lift was big and broad, with sharp, pointed ears. It lunged to its feet. David dropped to his knees, grabbed Scrub's muzzle, and stifled the glad bark. "No!" he whispered. "Be quiet! Quiet!"

Scrub whined and pawed at David in a frenzy of excitement. He thrust his head against David and the boy scratched his ears. The moment he let go of Scrub's muzzle, the dog began licking his face and whimpering. David opened the sack of scraps, sat in the snow, and fed Scrub. While the dog gobbled down the food, the boy's hands explored over his body. "You're thin," he whispered. "I can feel your ribs. But your muscles are hard as rock."

Scrub waved his tail wildly, whined, and shoved his head against David's chest. "I miss you, too," David whispered. He held the dog's head between his hands and pressed his face against the cold, furry forehead. The unusual activity and the boy's whispering roused the other dogs. They began to stand up and watch. Any moment one might bark and set off the whole bunch.

David patted Scrub and whispered, "I've got to go now. I'll come again soon." He hurried off toward the brush.

Before he'd got halfway Scrub's long, mournful howl rose in the night. David glanced back. Scrub was sitting on his tail, nose pointed at the stars, while he poured out his grief at being left behind. David started back to try to quiet him. The cabin door flew open, and Jackson emerged with the ever-handy whip. "Shut up," he shouted. "Shut up."

Scrub paid no attention. Jackson yelled again. Then he ran at the dog cursing. He lashed him with the whip and Scrub's howls of grief turned to howls of pain. He dodged about, trying to escape, but the short chain hampered him, and Jackson's aim was perfect. The lash was cutting unmercifully, and the man was shouting with every swing.

Hardly aware of what he was doing, David rushed at Jackson. He charged into the man full-tilt from behind and sent him sprawling. He grabbed the whip with both hands and tried to tear it loose. Jackson struggled to his feet, dragging David with him. He was much too strong for the boy. He tore the whip from David's hands, and his big fist crashed into the boy's face and knocked him backward into the snow.

David staggered up, sick and dizzy. The taste of blood was in his mouth. He dived for the whip. Again, Jackson's fist smashed him back in the snow. David tried to get up, but all strength was gone from his arms and legs. He heard Scrub snarling and lunging at his chain. The excitement had got to the rest of the team. They added their voices to the din.

David rolled onto his back and tried to sit up. That

moment the lash exploded in his face. It felt like a white hot iron had been forced against his cheek. He threw his hands over his face to protect his eyes. The lash came again and again. He felt the sting through the backs of his mittens and the thickness of the parka across his chest and shoulders. Jackson was beating him as he would one of his dogs. Under the rain of blows David got shakily to his feet.

Jackson's hands gripped him. His perpetually grinning face was shoved close. The reek of whiskey was on his breath. "You sneakin' half-breed. Come to steal my dog."

"I only came to see him," David managed.

"Tryin' to steal my dog." Jackson's open hand slashed across his face. "I ever catch you here again, I'll kill you."

He hurled David from him, and the boy sprawled in the snow. He scrambled up and stumbled away.

Scrub began to mourn his departure at the top of his lungs. Then came the crack of the whip. Scrub's mourning turned to howls of pain again. David ran blindly through the night, trying to shut out the sound of Scrub's crying.

-7-

David's face was on fire when he reached home. He looked at himself in the mirror and was shocked. His mouth was bloody and swollen. A couple of front teeth felt loose. The whip had split the skin across the bridge of his nose and both cheeks. Blood oozed from the cut. An inch higher and he could have lost an eye or both eyes.

He washed his face in cold water. It helped, but it didn't stop the burning. He got a pan of snow and sat at the kitchen table holding handfuls against the bruises.

Gradually the burning subsided.

He studied his face again. He didn't want his parents to know what had happened. His father would half-kill Jackson, and he'd be angry with David because of his stupid act.

The swelling around his mouth would probably go down before his parents returned. Somewhere he'd read that loose teeth often tightened up again. The whip slash across his face bothered him most. That gash was too deep to heal in a hurry. It was going to be visible for some time. It would be well scabbed over. But it would look bad.

David wondered if he'd have a scar like Jackson's. There'd be questions, particularly from his mother. He had to come up with a logical story. He considered saying that he slipped while carrying in wood and struck his face against the stove. But his mother would pick that story apart in no time. Maybe he could say a chunk had flown off the ax when he was cutting firewood. But chunks didn't fly when you were splitting block wood.

Finally he hit upon a story he was sure would do. While hiking through the brush, a limb snapped back and struck him across the face. That was logical. Even his father couldn't find fault with that one. At one time or another it had happened to everyone who got out into the woods. He'd never known of anyone getting such a deep gash that way. But several times he'd been stung enough to raise a welt. His cuts should be healed well enough by the time they returned so they'd accept the story.

The next day David was back on the hill, crouched behind the rock. He watched Jackson and the team go by, heading home. Scrub seemed none the worse for his beating.

David worked out a routine for his days. The daylight hours in winter were short, so there was little he could do outside. After breakfast he did the dishes, cleaned up the kitchen, and made his bed. He spent an hour at the woodpile splitting blocks and piling the stove wood on the back porch. He wanted enough to last his mother the week he was gone. The snow was getting deep on the roof. He knocked off a lot with a long pole. Another day was spent clearing the snow off the doghouses. After that, he took hikes and did a lot of reading in the evening. He'd have gone to visit Nick and Jean at Aurora, but he didn't want them to see his face.

One thing he never missed, the pilgrimage to the hill to watch Scrub go by. He was beginning to make a good lead dog, David told himself. In fact, the whole team was improving. It seemed they pulled the load of logs easier and faster.

A dozen times a day David studied his face in the mirror. The swelling was slowly disappearing. By the fifth day his mouth, lips, and cheeks were back to normal. Surprisingly, the two teeth tightened again. The whip cuts were scabbed over, but they'd be much in evidence when his parents returned.

It was the evening of the sixth day, and he was reading in the kitchen, when he heard the dogs. He threw open the door, and there was the team pulling up at the porch. His mother shouted happily, "David, hello, hello!" and started climbing out of the basket. Then she saw his face. "What happened to you?"

David told her about the hike and the snapping limb. "It hurt at first, but it's about healed up now."

She looked closely. "I can imagine. That was deep. You could have lost an eye or both eyes."

His father asked, "What were you doing, dreaming along?"

"I guess so. All I know is suddenly I got hit."

"It's a wonder boys live to grow up," Fred said. "Keep your wits about you. A thing like that can be serious out here." He began to unhitch the team. "Anything happen while we were gone?"

"Everything was quiet."

"You made out all right?" his mother asked. "You didn't get lonesome?"

"A little. But it wasn't bad. How'd you do?"

"I enjoyed it." She gathered up the rifle and blankets and went inside.

David helped his father with the dogs. There'd been no probing questions. They believed him. When the dogs were staked out, his father said, "You go on in, it's cold out here. I'll unload the sled."

His mother was out of her parka and looking around the kitchen. Her cheeks were flushed from the cold. "You're a pretty good housekeeper. I can see I won't have to worry about coming home to a mess."

"I took lessons from you. It's easier to keep house here than on the trail."

"Much easier. But the trail is fun. It's such a change." She leaned against the sink and folded her arms. "Now let's have the truth about your face."

He was startled. "Mom, I told you."

She shook her head. "It would have to be a very small limb to make such a narrow scab. A limb that

86

small snapping back would sting but it wouldn't be strong enough to cut that deep."

"I should know."

"You do, and that's not it. Besides, you've never been a good liar. Now do I start guessing?"

He hadn't fooled her at all. "I suppose you've figured it out," he said.

"I can come close."

"I sneaked up to see Scrub and ran into Smiley Jackson." He told her quickly what had happened. She listened, her lips pulled into a straight line, her black eyes snapping.

"He had a right to run you off," Celia said angrily, "but not to use a whip on you as if you were one of his dogs. For two cents I'd go up there and—and scalp that drunken bum."

"Mom!" David said, shocked.

"Well, that's what us Indians are famous for, isn't it? He could have blinded you for life."

"It's over. Let's just forget it."

"We'll have to, this time. We can't let your father know. But it better not happen again."

"Do you think Dad will guess?" he asked, worried.

"He would if he paid close attention, but his mind's on trapping and fur. Besides," she smiled and her burst of anger blew away, "few fathers know their sons as well as I do you. Now I want your solemn promise to keep completely away from Jackson's place and Scrub, or I won't leave you here alone again."

"I promise," David said. "All I did was get Scrub a beating, too."

Fred rested a day during which he did a little work on the sled and repaired one of the dogs' harnesses.

The following day he was ready to leave again, and it was David's turn to go along.

Celia waved from the porch. "You fellows be careful," she called.

"Sure," Fred answered. "Keep the home fires burning. Dave left you plenty of wood."

Fred again suggested David try handling the team. "If we're going to lengthen this line and you run part of it, you've got to learn to handle a dog team."

"They're used to you, not me. Maybe I can't."

"Nonsense. Five-year-old kids have handled three-dog teams in junior races. It's time you got over some of this timidity. You'll be doing a man's work next year and will need a team."

It was not that he was afraid. But he'd always seen men behind these big teams. To handle one would be like stepping out in competition with men. He didn't feel up to that.

"Come on. Try it." Fred stepped off the runners, went around, and got in the basket.

David took his stance on the runners and got a good grip on the handles. The team waited expectantly. Noble looked back at him. David made his voice as much like his father's as possible and yelled, "Noble, let's go!"

The sled shot away. David lost his grip and tumbled

88

into the snow. Fred shouted from the basket, "Noble!" and the big dog turned and came back to David. "Get a tighter grip," his father advised. "Lean forward as the sled starts."

David took a firm grip again and shouted. This time he was ready for the expected rush. The sled took off and he rode with it. This was different from riding bundled up in the basket. Every bump and imperfection in the trail came up through his feet and threatened to upset him. Wind shouldered against him. The sled drifted to the right, then to the left. This called for balance and all his strength. The forward speed of the sled and his precarious position forced him to stay alert. They made a sharp turn to avoid a hidden rock. He was not braced and fell again. He was dumped twice in the next hour. Then Fred took over.

After that David took his turn handling the team. By the fourth day he felt fairly secure on the runners.

The long, limber lash was the one thing he was unable to manage. It was hard to balance on the speeding runners and use the whip. He caught it on the brush, or the lash hit a rock or stump. Sometimes he didn't swing his arm forward hard enough, or he hurried the swing because he'd almost lost his balance. Then the lash fell into the snow. Once he actually hit himself. When it did curl over the dog's backs, he had no idea where the end would pop.

"You need practice," Fred said. "There's an old whip hanging on the wall of the fur house at home. Practice with that. Just remember, the idea is not to use the whip on the dogs. It's to keep them eager, to let them know you're behind them and have everything under control. It's a signal, or warning if a fight's about to break out. When that happens, use the butt of the whip to break it up."

David was handling the team when they pulled into Scotty's the fifth night.

"So," Scotty said, "we've got a new musher. How're you doing, Davie?"

"I don't know," David said.

"He's doing fine," Fred said. "No problems he can't lick."

Scotty helped them unhitch and stake out the dogs. They had almost finished, when he asked, "What did Jackson do with my friend, Scrub?"

"He's Jackson's lead dog," Fred said.

"You don't say." Scotty scratched his head with the hook and watched Fred unhitch and stake out the last dog. "Got a hunch that dog could make a good leader. That is, if Jackson don't up and spoil 'im. Well, let's go inside before we freeze to death standing here."

Once again they pulled in at home with a good catch. Fred was happy. He said to Celia, "This is going to be a fine harvest. And you ought to see Dave handle the team. We'll pick up some more dogs next summer for him and lengthen the line."

"You think David's ready?" she asked.

"He's almost ready now. What do you say, Dave?"

"I'd like it fine, if I can do it," Dave said.

"You will," Fred said.

Fred spent his usual day at home and was ready to take off again. It was Celia's turn to go. She gave David a warning look as she settled in the basket. "You be careful, hear?"

"I will," he promised.

"Don't forget to practice with that old whip," Fred said, and they were off.

David spent long hours with the whip. He carried it with him on hikes, popping it at twigs, stumps, rocks. Everything was a target. His accuracy increased until he could shatter an icicle hanging from the edge of the roof the full length of the whip away.

Every day he climbed the hill to watch from behind the rock for Scrub and the team to struggle past with the load of logs. There was steady improvement. Scrub moved out with confidence and strength. He kept the team strung out. Now Jackson was letting him set his own pace. Scrub had a sharp eye for obstacles in the trail and he tended strictly to business. Each day they passed around the base of the hill and disappeared, running fast and well. As much as he hated Jackson, David had to admit he was rounding the team into top racing condition.

Toward the end of the week the scab across his face dropped off. There was no scar.

A month passed. David was home again. It was the last day he'd be alone, and he barely made the top of the hill to watch for Scrub and the team, when he saw them. They were coming from a different direction.

Their excited yapping drowned out Jackson's voice. They skimmed over the snow at a speed he'd never seen before. Then, as they drew near, he saw why. The load of logs was gone. The dogs were running light and fast. They were happy. That meant Jackson considered the training period at an end.

The team of dogs did not round the base of the hill and disappear, as usual. This time, the dogs turned sharply and headed straight out across the snow-blanketed tundra. For a moment David was surprised. Then he understood what the change of direction, the light sled meant.

Smiley Jackson was leaving Aurora. He was heading for the first of a series of small races that would give the team the experience of running in competition. Eventually, if they were lucky, they'd end up at the Fur Rendezvous in Anchorage, the North American Championships at Fairbanks, or both.

David felt his throat go dry. This was probably the last time he would ever see Scrub, even from a distance. His friend was going away straight into a brittle sun that hung low on the horizon. David watched until his eyes watered. The team and Jackson became smaller and smaller until they were like a tiny Eskimo carving on the immense landscape. David could not distinguish Scrub at all.

- 8 -

Winter clamped an icy fist on the land. The snow depth increased. Fred estimated the river ice was three feet thick. The moose disappeared from their area, and David and Fred ran across a herd miles away yarded up in a cleared spot where the snow was not so deep and it was easier for them to move about. The caribou came. The ptarmigans arrived in flocks at the lower levels to winter in the willows.

David and Celia still took turns going out on the trap line. David now handled the team almost half the time when he was out with his father. Constant practice had made him very good with the long whip.

They glimpsed wolves many times, but the animals were almost instantly gone. The more the winter advanced and the colder it became, the more wolves they seemed to see and hear. They were skinning the day's catch in the number two cabin one night, when a sound brought David's head up with a jerk and goose bumps popped out on his arms. Wolves seemed to be all around them. He had heard individual wolves howl before, but never a chorus like this. It began low, and rose soaring into the frigid silence. He could even distinguish individual voices. Some were high and piercing, others low and soft. They blended into one wild harmony that filled the night. The sound faded and vanished, and the silence was greater than before. Then it started up again.

Fred looked up from skinning a marten and smiled, "Wolves singing. Pretty, isn't it?"

David said, almost in a whisper, "It sounds like a hundred. I've never heard anything like this."

"They wouldn't come this close to a settlement like Aurora. There might be a dozen out there."

"What about the dogs?"

"Nothing to worry about. Those wolves are enjoying themselves. They wouldn't be putting on a concert if they were hungry."

David thought of Scrub often. He wondered where he was and how the team was doing in the small races Jackson would be entering. During his week at home, he began hiking to Nick and Jean Moore's at Aurora. The couple took the Anchorage paper, delivered once a week by bush pilot. The race results were usually listed. Nick was caretaker at the mine during the winter. He ran a short trap line on the side on snowshoes because he had no dog team. Jean was small, grayhaired, and friendly.

At first there were no announcements of Smiley Jackson's team. Then one week, they were listed in third place at Echo Lake. The next report stated they'd won a second place. Then they won two firsts in a row. A reporter had added a line at the bottom of the last announcement. "Keep an eye on this Jackson team. It's young and inexperienced. But Jackson has a lead dog he calls Scrub who looks like a comer. He's big, strong, and fast."

David yelled excitedly, "Jean, look! Look!"

Jean read the short article and smiled. "How about that! It looks like Scrub's doing all right. Who'd have believed he'd turn out like this when he was thieving everything he could get his teeth into around here?"

"Maybe that's what made him fast," David said. "He had to run to live."

"Could be. Anyhow, he just might put Aurora on the map. Now wouldn't that be something?"

Two weeks later the first blizzard of the winter hit. David and Fred had arrived home early that evening. The wind was building, shaking snow from the trees and swirling it through the air. The thermometer fell steadily. Fred looked at the lowering sky. He turned his face to the wind. "I've a feeling it would be a good idea to cut a lot of wood and stack it on the porch."

They spent all the next morning splitting blocks and piling wood on the porch until there was only an alleyway to walk through.

By evening the first fine snowflakes were falling. David awoke in the middle of the night. He was cold, and wind was howling at the sturdy corners of the cabin. He got out of bed and went to the window. Frost was a quarter-inch thick on the glass. He held his palm against the frost until he'd melted a round spot to look through. There were no stars or moon. He could not see the sky. He could not even see the doghouses. Fine snow scudded so thickly across the frozen earth it seemed the land was moving. He got another blanket, spread it over his bed, and crawled in. He lay listening to the wind. The dogs would be all right in their houses and with their thick coats. There were two bales, three thousand pounds, of dried fish stored in the fur cabin. His father would not go out on the trap line until the blizzard passed. He wondered how long it would last.

With morning, the world was closed in a swirling mass of snow that pelted the cabin like fine shot. Cold cut through the thickest winter clothing when they went out to feed the dogs. Even with daylight, the doghouses were barely visible. Snow drifted against them, building mounds that left just the black hole of the opening clear. Not a dog was in sight. The thermometer on the porch registered fifty-five below zero and was still falling.

"It's going to hit bottom sure," Fred predicted. Bottom was sixty. "There'll be little fur next trip. Every living thing has hunted a hole until this blows over."

The thermometer hit bottom, then slowly rose to fifty-five, and hung there day after day. The icy air was constantly filled with pelting, fine snow. The wind picked it off the frozen earth and drifted it against every conceivable obstruction—a protruding rock, bush, stump, a mound of earth. The snow even built tiny mounds against single, dead grass-blades. The roof of the cabin was blown clear of snow. In back, snow drifted halfway to the eaves and made that wall warmer than any other.

They kept the fire going night and day. By the end of the week, they had burned all the wood piled on the porch. David and Fred went into the storm and dug down through the drift to the woodpile. They dared not work fast and were particularly careful to breathe slowly and shallowly. A few careless deep breaths could frost the lungs and kill. All day they huddled about the stove soaking up the warmth. At night Celia piled on the blankets. She heated two big rocks on top of the stove for David's bed, wrapped them in newspapers, and shoved them under the covers. Several times during the night, David was wakened by his father stoking the stove.

During the tenth night, David thought the voice of the wind was a little less violent. He melted a peep-hole in the window and peered out. Snow was still scudding across the yard. He could not see the sky or doghouses. It was wishful thinking. When he awoke again, it was still dark. But something was different. Then he realized the wind had stopped.

He heard Fred's glad shout from the kitchen, "Roll out everybody. The storm's over!"

David dressed swiftly and joined his parents.

"Come on," Fred said, "let's have a look at the world

we've got." They went out on the porch together. The clearing was blown almost bare, but snow was piled four and five feet deep against obstructions they couldn't even see. The air was clear and still. Compared to what it had been, thirty below and no wind felt almost balmy. Every bush and tree had been blown clean. They stood upright in black silhouette against a white world. A covey of ptarmigans sailed over the clearing. A snowshoe rabbit popped out of the brush, hopped a few feet, and disappeared again. Wildlife was coming out to feed.

The dogs were all out sitting on their tails in front of their snow-covered houses. Noble barked his happiness that the storm was ended.

"I've got to get moving fast," Fred said. "It's been eleven days since I've been on the line." He looked at Celia. "Maybe you'd better stay home this trip. It's going to be rough."

"I know all about that. I was born in this country. Remember? The blankets and everything else in the cabins will be frozen stiff. There'll be a couple of inches of snow on the floor where it drifted through cracks and Lord knows what else. I'm going. This time you'll really need help. Besides, it's my turn."

"The trail will be drifted over, too. It'll be hard traveling."

"So, who's afraid of a little old storm?"

"Just remember I gave you a chance to back out."

"Who wants it?" Celia said.

They rushed about, getting ready. David helped his father hitch up the dogs. An hour later Celia was snug in the basket, surrounded by blankets and holding the rifle. She shouted, "Take care, David."

His father lifted a hand. "See you next week, Dave. Let's go, Noble." The whip cracked. The dogs lunged into the harnesses, yapping excitedly. They were happy to be on the trail again.

David washed the dishes and cleaned up the house. He spent the rest of the forenoon chopping wood and piling a great rick on the porch again. In the afternoon he hiked to Nick and Jean Moore's to search the Anchorage papers for any dog-racing news that might mention Jackson and Scrub. There was none.

For four days the good weather held. The fifth morning a new storm boiled out of the north and hit them. As Fred would have said, "The old one just backed up for a new start." Wind howled at the corners of the cabin. Snow swept across the frozen earth to add to the drifts already formed. Again the thermometer hit bottom. David didn't stir out except to bring in more wood.

The storm lasted three days, then blew itself out as quickly as it had begun. Again there was silence. The thermometer rose to twenty below and stayed there.

Fred and Celia did not return, but David hadn't expected them. They'd have holed up in one of the cabins until the storm broke.

The middle of the eighth day David was preparing

to go out to cut more wood, when he heard dogs barking.

He threw open the door, and there was Noble leading the team into the clearing, tongue hanging out, tail waving, happy to be home again.

His mother was not bundled up in the basket. The musher was not his father. The figure riding the runners lifted a steel hook in greeting. Scotty's voice shouted, "Davie! Davie!"

David jumped off the porch, and Noble rushed up to him. "Scotty! Where's Mom and Dad? How come you've got the team?"

"It's quite a story. Help me unhitch. Then we'll go inside, and I'll tell you about it."

"They're staying at your place?"

"In a manner of speakin'. Help me with the dogs, Davie."

David was bursting with questions, but he helped unhitch the team and stake the dogs to their houses. They went inside, and Scotty got out of his parka. He sat in a chair and motioned to another, "Sit down, Davie."

David sat and waited. He'd never seen Scotty so sober.

Scotty rubbed his hand over the hook on his left arm. He ran fingers through his hair. He seemed at a loss to begin. "This was a bad storm," he said finally. "Bad as we've had in a long time. That second one coming so soon was a real fooler."

A cold finger probed in David's vitals. "Scotty, Mom

100

and Dad are all right, aren't they? You said they were at your place."

"Don't rush me, Davie. I'm doin' the best I know how. Like I said, this was a bad storm. Your mom and dad didn't come and they didn't come. Right in the middle of that second blow, I heard the dogs, and there they was standin' outside the cabin all alone. I started back right off, lookin' for your ma and pa. I found 'em huddled behind a big rock in the snow. They'd tried to make it back to number three cabin, but they were still a couple of miles away."

"Then they're all right." The cold finger stopped probing. "They're at your place."

Scotty shook his head. His eyes were sick. "I took 'em to my place. They're not all right, Davie. They was both froze to death when I found 'em."

The words had no meaning. They were stones dropped into a quiet pool. He watched them sink and sink through crystal depths.

Scotty's voice went on and on. "Maybe they had stopped to rest. Something spooked the dogs and they took off, leaving your ma and pa. Maybe the sled hit a rock or stump or somehow went over a bank and spilled them out, knocking one, or both of them out. And the dogs went on when nobody yelled to stop. They could have been workin' at a set, and the dogs took out after a moose, a rabbit, or a fox. So many things could have happened. If there was ever any clues to what went wrong, the storm wiped 'em out or covered 'em up. All I know for sure is that somehow they became separated from the team. They tried to make it back to cabin number three and didn't. The team came on to my place because they always have."

"They're dead," David whispered. "They're both dead." He began to shake. He gripped the edge of the chair as if he were falling.

Scotty put his arms around him and held him close. Then David began to cry.

The following days were a nightmare that Scotty led David through gently but firmly. It was Scotty who brought his parents back. Scotty made arrangements for the funeral. Through shortwave at the trading post, he got in touch with David's uncle, George Martin, in Anchorage. Uncle George came out by bush pilot. David had seen his uncle twice in his life. Both times when he had come to visit for a couple of days.

Uncle George was not as big as his father. But he had the same lean features and was rawboned and dark. He had worked in one of the airports somewhere in the state of Washington and was transferred to Anchorage a little over a year ago. He held some kind of office job.

After the funeral, Uncle George said, "David, I want you to come live with your aunt Margaret and me. You've never met your cousins, Terry and Grace, but they're near your age and will be good company for you."

"I don't want to leave here."

"You can't live alone. Can he, Scotty?"

"I was on my own at his age. But I can tell you it's pretty lonesome."

"I'm sure Fred and Celia would want David to live with us."

"What about his mother's people?" Scotty asked. "He's got uncles and aunts on that side of the family."

"Do you know where they are?"

"Not right off or I'd have notified 'em. They fish along the coast and move about a lot. In time they could be located."

"His parents wouldn't want David living that kind of nomad existence. He'll come to Anchorage."

"That all right with you, Davie?" Scotty asked. "You want to live with your father's people?"

David felt numb and lost. They were talking about him, planning his future life, but it seemed like it was someone else. It didn't matter. Uncle George was his uncle. He had taken charge and was making decisions. He guessed someone had to.

"It's all right," David said.

"I need Davie to help me for a few days," Scotty said. "We've got to go over the line and take up all the traps. He knows where they are. I don't. And we've got to move the fur stored here to my place, where I can keep it for him."

"How long will that take?"

"Give us ten days. There must be over five hundred traps, and there'll be fur to skin out and care for."

"Shall we say ten days from tomorrow? Good. I'll send the bush pilot back for David. What disposition

103

do we make of all these things that are left, the traps, the fur, the house and furnishings?"

"I can probably sell the traps and maybe the trap line next spring or summer. When the fur buyers come around next spring, I'll sell the fur and send you the money. There should be six or seven thousand dollars in fur alone. You can put it in the bank for Davie. I might sell the cabin to the person who buys the trap line. Otherwise, out here you just lock the door and walk away." He turned to David. "I'll look after it, in case you ever want to come back. There's one other thing, Davie—Nick and Jean Moore have offered to keep the team for you. Do you want to give them the dogs, or shall I try to sell 'em?"

"Give them to the Moores," David said.

"I guess that covers everything," Uncle George said. "I'm sorry to be loading you down with work, Scotty. Deduct whatever expenses you have and take what you think is right as pay for your time and trouble."

"No trouble," Scotty said. "These are my friends."

David's future was arranged and he had scarcely listened.

The next ten days were hard for David. Finding the traps and taking them up was no problem. But there were so many memories along the line. He remembered the night at cabin number two when he and his father listened to the wolves singing. There was his first attempt at mushing. His father's patience with him in handling the team and teaching him how to make sets. And somewhere beyond cabin number three was the rock behind which his parents had crouched and frozen to death. But he didn't ask Scotty where it was.

When they finally made Scotty's cabin, they were loaded down with traps and fur. They cleaned out the spare room and left everything. Then they went on to David's home, where they loaded up with fur again. It required two trips to transport all the fur to Scotty's.

"It's a right nice harvest," Scotty observed, surveying the pile in his back room. "We'll sell a few pelts to the trading post now, so you can have some walk-around money."

"Walk-around money?"

"Spendin' money. Pocket money. There's things you'll wanta buy in the city."

"How much money?"

"Depends. I think you should give your uncle and aunt a couple hundred dollars for takin' care of you. Then you'll need clothes and I don't know what all. Say somewhere between four and five hundred dollars. Come spring I'll sell your fur and send the money to you. You and your uncle can have a lawyer in Anchorage fix it up all legal to pay your relatives so much a month or year as long as you stay."

The fur they sold brought four hundred and fifty dollars. It was more money than David had ever had in his life before.

Nick and Jean Moore came for the dogs. "Remember, Dave, they're yours any time you want them," Nick said. "We'll just be keeping them for you."

"Thanks." David patted Noble's big head and

scratched his ears. Noble licked his hand. He was a good dog—smart, gentle, and loyal. And he'd been kind to Scrub. David felt guilty that he didn't feel loss at leaving him.

The plane came for him about noon. It dropped into the clearing on skis and ran up to the cabin where David and Scotty waited. David had his few clothes in his father's old knapsack.

Scotty shook his hand. "I'll come over every so often and check on the cabin. If you ever want anything, anything at all, you know where I live. You remember that."

"I will."

The plane's motor was still turning over. The cabin door was open. The pilot waited. This was the moment he'd been dreading and refusing to face for ten days. He looked around. The Moores had already taken the doghouses. The cabin door was locked, the curtains drawn. No smoke curled from the chimney. Already it looked forlorn and deserted. He knew what would happen with no one here to care for it. The roof would eventually cave in from rot, the walls collapse. His parents' possessions would mold and rot. In a few years the forest would grow over the clearing and claim the cabin for its own. All signs that a family had lived and worked and dreamed here would be gone. Something came up in his throat and began to choke him.

The pilot asked, "Ready, son?"

Scotty said, "Good luck. Take care, Davie."

106

He couldn't answer. He got into the plane and closed the door.

The pilot said, "Fasten your seat belt, son."

They roared through the snow and shot upward into the clear sky. The plane banked and thundered over the cabin. The small figure in the clearing lifted the stub of his arm in farewell.

David had never been in a modern city like Anchorage. When he broke his leg, his parents had taken him to a doctor in one of the small interior towns.

Uncle George met him at the airport. They drove through the city's downtown traffic and out into the residential section. Halfway down a street they turned into a driveway.

"Here we are," Uncle George said cheerfully. "Home."

The house was two stories tall. It was one of the biggest, and David thought, the nicest-looking house on the block. His uncle led him into the living room.

"Margaret," Uncle George called, "David's here."

His aunt came from the kitchen. She was tall and thin. She had the blondest hair he'd ever seen piled on her head in glistening coils. Her eyes were big and very blue. She shook his hand, smiling. "David! I've been looking forward to meeting you."

David said, "Yes, ma'am."

She kept smiling at him. "That's quite a get-up

108

you're wearing. You look like an Eskimo or an Indian in it."

"My mother was Indian," David said.

"I wasn't thinking of that, David. You know, George," she said, "if he got rid of those boot things, what are they—mukluks—and the parka and got some more conventional clothing: a jacket, some sweaters, and shoes—"

"A lot of Anchorage people dress this way in winter, Margaret. I see nothing wrong with it."

"I know it," Aunt Margaret said. "And I still say out in the bush it's fine, but not in the city. You don't happen to have anything else to wear in that bag, do you, David?"

"Some shirts and socks," David said.

"If clothing just weren't so expensive," she mused.

David remembered his money and brought out his wallet. "I can buy my own clothes. We sold a little fur before I left." He extracted two hundred and fifty dollars and handed it to his uncle. "This is to help pay for my keep until Scotty sells the furs and traps in the spring. Then I'll give you more."

His uncle pushed the money aside. "You're my brother's son, David. We're happy to have you."

"I can take it." Aunt Margaret held out her hand, and David gave her the money.

"Margaret!" Uncle George said angrily, "I will not take from my brother's boy."

"Just a minute," Aunt Margaret said calmly. "I'm glad to have David, too. I hope he understands that.

But he has it to give and he wants to. We have two children of our own to support and we're not exactly rich. If David didn't have it, that would be different. Besides, this will give him a feeling of independence, of paying his own way and not accepting charity. Isn't that right, David?"

"Scotty and I talked it over," David said to his uncle. "I want to do this."

"Well," Uncle George rubbed his face with an angry gesture that was like David's father, "all right. But I don't like it."

Aunt Margaret said, "Show David his room, George. Then suppose you two go downtown and get him some new clothes, the kind we'd get Terry." She explained to David, "Your room's not big and it's not furnished as well as I'd like. But after living out in the bush so long, I don't imagine you'll mind."

"For the love of mike!" Uncle George said angrily, "Fred didn't live primitive."

"Really?" Aunt Margaret's blue eyes were surprised. "You had electricity, running water, and that sort of thing?"

"No," David said.

"There, you see," she said to his uncle.

Uncle George shook his head and said, "Come on, David." They climbed the narrow, winding stairs single file. The room was under the roof. David could stand upright in the middle but not on the sides where the roof sloped. A single window looked out over the city.

There was a bunk bed, a small dresser, and a stand with a bed lamp. One wall was a clothes closet. There was a small rug in front of the bed.

"I'm sorry it's not better," Uncle George said. "We never thought we'd use it."

"This is fine," David said.

"About your aunt, David. She always lived in the city. She was born and raised in an apartment. She was never more than a few blocks from a beauty parlor until we moved up here. She won't get out and see the country, but sticks to downtown. A moose did come down the street a month ago and chased a couple of people indoors. Now Margaret will hardly walk around the neighborhood. She thinks the minute you get out of the city limits you're back in the Alaska of 1898. Apparently it's going to take a lot of time for her to adjust."

"Sure," David said.

"Now let's go downtown and get those clothes."

The store they went into had nothing but men's clothing. David had never seen so many varieties and colors. There were whole racks of pants, coats, jackets of all kinds. Shirts and sweaters were stacked in piles on counters. There was a counter of nothing but socks, another of brightly colored ties. The walls were lined from floor to ceiling with hundreds of boxes of shoes.

Uncle George began pawing through a rack of pants. "See anything here you like?"

David said, bewildered, "I like it all."

Uncle George smiled. "Want me to pick out a couple of pairs of pants for you?"

"You pick it all out. I wouldn't know where to start."

"Shoes, a couple of pairs of pants, a jacket, shirts, and sweaters will make a hundred dollars look sick," Uncle George warned.

"I've got enough."

A clerk approached, and Uncle George explained what they wanted. The clerk nodded. "The works, eh?"

In no time David was decked out in new shoes, pants, a sweater, stocking cap, and fleece-lined jacket. It all came to ninety-six dollars. David looked at himself in a full-length mirror. "I sure look different."

The salesman smiled. "They do say clothes make the man." David's parka and old clothing went into a bag, and they left the store.

When they reached home his cousins, Grace and Terry, were there from school. Terry was about a year younger than David and not as tall. He was thin and blond like his mother, and had her blue eyes. He looked David over, said, "Hi, Dave," and was through with him.

Grace was just the opposite. She was about eleven, David guessed, a little chubby, and her smile was big and friendly. "Hi, Davie," she grinned. Then she looked disappointed. "Gee, I thought you'd look like somebody getting ready to go to the North Pole or something. But you look like everybody else."

"I think you look fine," Aunt Margaret said. "The new clothes are a real improvement."

112

David said to Grace, "My parka and mukluks are in the bag. I just bought these clothes."

"Can I see 'em?"

"Sure." David handed her the package. Grace untied it and lifted out the parka. "Wow, what a beauty!" She started to slip it over her head.

"Hey, don't do that," Terry warned. "You don't know what kind of dirt it's been in. Dave's been wearing it all over."

"I wear it outside and only in winter," David said. "Parkas don't get dirty in snow and forty below."

Grace paid no attention. She got into the parka, which reached well below her knees. She stood in front of the mirror admiring herself.

Aunt Margaret watched.

"It looks fine on you, honey," Uncle George said.

"It's a mile too big," Terry said.

"I could cut the bottom off," Grace said, turning around. "And if I wore three or four sweaters underneath, it'd almost fit." She smiled at David. "I won't, of course. Cut it off, I mean. But I'd sure like to have one." She slipped out of it and handed it back to David.

David took the parka and package and headed upstairs.

"Hurry up, David," his aunt said. "Dinner's ready."

During dinner Grace asked, "You going to start school right away, Davie?"

"I don't know," David glanced at Uncle George. "I hadn't thought about it."

"Margaret and I talked it over," Uncle George said,

"and since you'd be entering high school, we thought it would be better to wait until next fall. You'd be coming into the middle of a term now. That's too much to make up."

"You had a school out there?" Terry asked with mock surprise. "You can read and write?"

"That's enough," Uncle George said sharply. "You're not funny."

"I think what Terry means is that he's surprised they'd have a school in such a small place as Aurora," Aunt Margaret said.

"Sure," Terry said, "you can hardly find it on a map."

"My teacher was a graduate of the University of Washington," David said. "We studied the same things and took the same exams you do here. I graduated from eighth grade last spring."

"You're smarter'n we are," Grace said. "I'm only in sixth and Terry's in eighth."

"I'll start high next fall, too," Terry said, "so you won't be ahead of me."

"Take it easy until next fall," his uncle said to David. "Wander around, get acquainted with the city, meet some of the people. Go to the library. Visit a couple of schools, if you like. Sort of get your feet on the ground and become oriented. Then next fall you'll be all set."

The talk at table was mostly what Grace and Terry were doing and the things that had happened during the day. The pond in Hunter's yard was frozen hard now, so Terry and his friends could ice-skate.

"You watch out for moose," Aunt Margaret said.

"Gosh, this is right in the yard. No moose'll come there."

→"One came right down this street a month or so ago and chased people," Aunt Margaret said. "It could happen again."

"Okay," Terry said, "I'll watch."

"Can you ice-skate, Davie?" Grace asked.

"No. There was too much snow on the river ice."

"What did you do for fun?" she asked.

David thought. "Not much, I guess. I hunted some in winter. In summer I fished in the river and hiked around the country."

"Didn't you have any friends to run around with?" she asked.

"We lived outside of Aurora," David said. "There were only ten other kids in school."

"Then you were alone most of the time," she said with quick sympathy.

"I guess so."

Uncle George told about a moose that had charged a neighbor's car on the road that morning. "Its horns punched a hole in the radiator and it smashed the hood before ambling off into the woods."

"You see," Aunt Margaret said, "practically in the city. And you say this isn't frontier."

"Did you have moose around your home?" Grace asked David.

"I watched a cow and her calf all summer," David said.

"That's nothing," Terry said, "we've seen moose tracks right here in the yard."

"It's downright dangerous to go out," Aunt Margaret said.

Uncle George smiled at David.

After dinner Grace and Aunt Margaret cleared the table and washed the dishes. David offered to help, but his aunt said, "We always do them together. Why don't you go into the living room and find something to read. We have a lot of magazines."

He found a magazine and settled into a chair. Uncle George was reading the paper. Terry had gone to his room to do homework. David turned the pages idly, listening to the murmur of the female voices from the kitchen. Finally that ceased and Grace and his aunt came into the living room. His aunt sat under one of the floor lamps and began crocheting on something that looked like a sweater.

Grace sat at the living-room table with an open math book, scowling and chewing the end of her pencil. She worked and scowled for a time. "Davie, did you have to take math?" she asked suddenly.

"Sure," David said.

Uncle George lowered the paper. "What's wrong, honey?"

"If a person pays ninety-seven fifty a year at the rate of six percent interest, how much has he borrowed? That's what's wrong."

"That's just principal times rate equals interest,

116

therefore interest divided by rate equals principal," David said.

"Clear as mud," Grace grumbled. "So who cares?"

"I can show you." David glanced at his uncle.

"Go ahead," he said, "just don't let her con you into working the whole problem for her. She's got to learn."

"Why?" Grace complained. "I'm not going to start out borrowing a whole bunch of money."

"We've been over that before," Uncle George said.

David pulled his chair up to the table and explained the problem. He stayed with Grace, pointing out mistakes and helping while she worked a dozen problems. "Okay, I guess I can do it," she said finally. "But I still don't like math."

An hour later Grace finished the rest of her homework, said good night, and went off to bed.

Uncle George had laid down the paper. David hunted through it for the dog-racing news. There was nothing about Smiley Jackson and Scrub. He told his uncle and aunt good night and went up to his attic room.

"If you get cold, there's more blankets in the bottom drawer of the dresser," his aunt called after him.

David took his old clothing from the bag and hung it in the closet. He counted his money—a hundred and four left. It seemed like a lot. When he considered the price of the clothing he'd bought today, he guessed it wasn't much to see him through until spring. He decided to put ninety dollars away and keep the fourteen in his wallet. He couldn't leave money lying out on top of the dresser. It should be put away. He finally stuffed it into the toe of one of his mukluks and put the shoes away in the closet.

He got into bed, but he could not sleep. The deep silence he had always known was gone. At intervals cars went by on the street. A door slammed. Voices called into the night. Somewhere a car was stuck in the snow, and the motor ground and ground. The stairwell was a funnel that brought his uncle's and aunt's voices up to him as clearly as if they were standing outside the door. They were talking about him.

"What do you think of David?" his uncle asked.

"I was hoping he wouldn't look so Indian."

"He's half."

"Why couldn't he look more like his father?"

"I think he's a rather good-looking boy."

"For an Indian, I suppose so."

"You can't call him an Indian."

"Maybe not technically," his aunt said, "but he certainly looks like one."

"That's why you wanted him to get different clothing, wasn't it?" Uncle George asked.

"It does make him look more like us, doesn't it?"

"Well, yes."

"I just can't understand what your brother was thinking of."

"Celia was a good-looking, intelligent woman, Margaret."

David pulled the covers over his head, so he'd hear

no more. He felt sick and lonely. He didn't know when he slept, but the next thing he knew it was morning.

After his uncle had left for work and Grace and Terry for school, David tried to make himself useful around the house. Maybe they'd get used to him being part Indian if he caused no extra work and could help out. He wiped the dishes for his aunt, made his own bed, then went outside and shoveled the snow off the walk and street in front of the house. After that there was nothing to do.

His aunt suggested, "Why don't you start getting acquainted with Anchorage, David? Take a walk. We'll have lunch at twelve."

David hiked the few blocks to the main business district. He wandered up and down the streets, amazed at the numbers of people. He peered into store windows, fascinated by the displays of clothing, jewelry, sporting goods, and tools. He stood for some time looking through the window of a restaurant, watching a cook making pancakes on a huge grill. Then he remembered Scotty's bacon pancakes and turned quickly away.

It was noon before he realized it. He hurried home. Uncle George had come for lunch, and the three of them ate together. Afterward David went up to his room for a while. But there was nothing to do. He became restless and went back downtown.

This time he found his way to the dock, where he saw his first oceangoing ship. He watched the loading and unloading of cargo a long time. Finally he returned to the business district. He was idling along, when he saw Terry standing in front of a hardware store, admiring a small shotgun in the window. He had a pair of ice skates slung over his shoulder.

David stopped beside him. "School out?" he asked.

"Yeah." Terry kept looking at the gun.

"Sure is a dandy," David said.

"It's been in the window for a couple of months," Terry said. "It's just right for ptarmigans and small game. I sure would like to have it." He glanced at David. "I guess you've got your own gun."

"I've got a rifle."

"I wouldn't have any use for a rifle. But I'd sure like to have that."

"If you're going home," David said, "I'll go with you."

"No, I—uh got to meet some fellows. You go on." Terry walked off.

A couple of blocks later, David saw Terry with three boys. They all carried ice skates.

David walked about a while longer, then headed for home. As he turned into the block, he heard shouting and laughter. Terry and his friends were skating on a sheet of ice in a nearby yard. Snow had been scraped away and water poured on the ground to form a small rink. David went over and stood watching. Terry didn't glance his way.

After a minute a tall boy skated over and said, "You can't stay here. This is private property."

120

"I just stopped to watch," David said. "Terry's my cousin."

The boy yelled, "Hey, Terry, the Indian says he's your cousin."

Terry skated over, his lips tight. "Quit following me around, Dave," he said.

"I wasn't following," David explained. "I was going home and saw you."

"Then go on. For pete's sake, find your own friends. There must be some Indians around town." The two boys skated away.

The tall one said, "I didn't know you had a half-breed relative."

"My uncle was stupid," Terry shot back.

David started forward, then stopped. He shoved his fists into his pockets and walked off.

A couple of nights later he was standing on a corner thinking it was about time to start home, when the school bus stopped and Grace got off. She waved at the kids and joined him on the sidewalk. "You going home, Davie?"

"Yes. Why?"

"I'll walk home with you." She smiled.

He didn't mean to say it but it just popped out, "You don't mind?"

"Walking home with you? Why should I? You're my cousin."

"Just thought you might," he said evasively.

"Why, Davie?"

"No reason."

She began walking backward in front of him, her small face framed in the hood serious. "Why?" she asked again.

"If you're not careful, you'll fall down."

"Because you're part Indian?" she asked. "Because you look like an Indian?"

He looked at her and said nothing.

"I heard those friends of Terry's talking at school. Terry's got some dopey friends. Don't you care what they say. I'm glad you're my cousin." She caught her heel and toppled over backward in a snowbank. Her schoolbooks went flying.

"I told you," David warned her.

She started to laugh and held out her hand.

David pulled her up and brushed her off. He cleaned the snow off her books and said, "I'll carry these. You drop them in the snow about once more and they'll be ruined."

As the days passed David made no friends his own age. The kids were all in school. There was no one to meet. He sat about the house and helped his aunt whenever possible. He spent hours wandering about the city and its outskirts. Grace alone kept the loneliness from becoming unbearable. Almost every night he helped her with math. In the afternoon he waited on the corner for her to get off the school bus. On these walks home he told her about Aurora, his home, his parents, the trap line, and Scotty. He told her what it was like to run a team of dogs through winter silence so deep it

122

made your ears ache. He told her about Scrub, not once, but many times. It helped ease his loneliness.

She asked once, "Will you ever go back, Davie?"

"I don't know," he said. "I'd like to."

"I hope you stay with us always," she said.

He smiled and reached for her load of books. "Let me carry those."

"I'd like to see your home and Aurora and everything," she said. "And I'd like to see Scrub. Don't you have any pictures of him?"

"I never owned a camera," David said. A minute later, they passed a jewelry store. He glanced in the window, then gripped Grace's arm. "That's Scrub! It looks just like him."

The object was a small Eskimo ivory carving of a sled dog. The figure stood braced on sturdy legs, head up, sharp ears pricked forward, bushy tail curved over its back.

"That's the way he used to stand and look at me," David smiled.

They squatted on their heels and stared through the window at the exquisitely carved dog.

"It's beautiful," Grace said. "I wish I had it. I'd put it on my dresser by the light where I could always look at it. No wonder you loved him."

"It costs fifteen dollars."

"I know."

They rose and went down the street. "I thought girls always wanted clothes and jewelry and things like that."

"I'll want them someday, when I get a lot older," Grace said practically. "But not now. I've always wanted a dog, but Mom says we can't keep one in the city. You've told me so much about Scrub that I feel like he's part mine, you being my cousin and all." She looked at him sideways. "You don't mind sharing him a little?"

"Not with you."

"Then I would like that ivory carving."

"I see," David said. But he didn't.

It snowed that night. The next morning he cleared the street and walk in front of the house. Then he went downtown. He was headed for the docks to watch a ship loading and was passing a clothing store, when a man said, "Hey, boy, you want a job?"

"A job?" David asked.

"Shovel the snow off the walk from here to the corner and I'll give you five dollars."

He wasn't half-through when the restaurant owner across the street asked him to do the same thing in front of his place. He did both jobs and made eight dollars that day.

That gave him an idea. Instead of spending his days aimlessly wandering the streets, he went from business to business asking if they had any jobs. He got no more snow-shoveling jobs, but some of them began hiring him for a few hours to work in the back of their stores. He cleaned up, helped uncrate merchandise, or ran errands. The money he made he stuffed into the toe of his mukluk, with his other bills. He tried to arrange his

124

jobs so he could meet Grace every night. If he wasn't on the corner waiting, she went home by bus. He was particularly late one night unpacking sports equipment in the hardware store.

On the way home he hesitated to admire the little ivory dog in the jewelry-store window. They were still open. On impulse he went in and said to a salesman, "Can I see that carving of a dog in the window?"

"It's fifteen dollars, son."

"I know."

The man hesitated. "If you break it, you'll have to pay for it. Can you do that?"

"Yes, sir."

"Well, all right." The salesman got the dog.

David turned it over in his hands. He felt the legs and the sharp ears. He looked into the face of the carving and visualized Scrub's amber eyes, the way the dog would look up into his face, and push his big head into his chest to have his ears scratched. He heard again the drum-hollow sound when he patted the deep chest. He remembered the day they learned to walk together. Fifteen dollars wasn't important; having the little ivory carving was.

He got out his purse and carefully counted out the money. "Will you wrap it up real good?"

"I'll put it in a box with cotton. You've got a nice carving there."

"Yes, sir," David said.

With the box in his pocket, he hurried home.

Dinner was over and Aunt Margaret and Grace had

125

cleared the table. His aunt said, "Good heavens, David, where have you been? We waited and waited. Uncle George was about to start out looking for you."

"I'm sorry," he said. "I was uncrating stuff at the hardware store. It took longer than I thought."

"You're working quite a lot." She looked at him closely. "You aren't broke, are you? I thought you had some left to tide you over until your friend sells your furs and traps."

"I have."

"That's fine," she said. "But try to get home in time for dinner after this."

Uncle George asked, "David, you aren't carrying all your money with you?"

"No, I left it in my room."

"Good. You could get your pockets picked or lose it."

Later when he went upstairs to his room, David unwrapped the little statue and put it on the night table beside the bed. He sat and looked at it, thinking about Scrub, wondering where he was, how many races he'd won, how he was, and if the dog remembered him. Somehow, as David looked at the little statue, Scrub didn't seem quite so far away.

- 10 -

One morning David saw men stringing a huge ANCHOR-AGE FUR RENDEZVOUS banner across the main street. An electric excitement gripped the city. This was the great Anchorage celebration he'd heard so much about, the carnival time of the year for the city. The highlight of the celebration would be the dog race. It drew the greatest teams from Alaska and beyond to compete for a cash prize of thousands of dollars. This was the race Smiley Jackson pointed for in the months he trained his team at Aurora. Scrub would be there!

David could hardly wait for Grace to get off the bus that night to tell her.

"Of course," she said, "school's going to close for the three-day celebration. Gee! Are you sure Scrub'll be here? I'll get to see him?"

"Sure," David said. "Smiley Jackson would never miss the big one."

They walked a block in silence. "I looked in that jewelry-store window the other day," Grace said. "The little ivory dog's gone."

It was on the tip of David's tongue to tell her he'd bought it, then for a reason he couldn't explain, he said, "I know."

A few days later the mushers began to arrive with their teams. They came into the city by truck and pickup, by train, and even by plane from north of the Arctic Circle. They mushed in from several hundred miles in the interior and from the southern part of Alaska. A dozen came from the Yukon Territory. Two came from the state of Washington and one from as far away as Massachusetts.

In all, thirty teams were there to fight for the big prize money and the honor of winning the greatest event in the north. When the paper published their names, that of Smiley Jackson was among them. His backer was one of the Anchorage stores.

The mushers and their teams were scattered throughout the city. David searched everywhere for Jackson. He asked other mushers, but at first no one seemed to know where the team from Aurora was staying.

Finally a young Eskimo said, "Smiley Jackson? Sure. Go to the end of the street. There's a trail leads outa town. Follow it about a mile through the brush, and you'll come to a little log cabin. He's holed up there."

David found the cabin. The dogs were staked out around it. There was a small, rotting shed at the edge of the brush about a hundred feet from the cabin. He crept to the shed and peeked around. The nearest dog was Scrub.

He stood broadside as David had seen him do so often. His big head was up, sharp ears pricked forward, plumed tail curved over his back. David studied him closely. He seemed broader of shoulder and deeper of chest. He looked strong and well-fed. His coat shone. He had a lead dog's air of confidence and authority. The whole team appeared to be in top condition.

David searched for signs of Jackson. No sound came from the cabin. No one passed before the small, curtainless window. No smoke issued from the stovepipe. Jackson must be downtown.

He stepped from behind the shed and started toward the dog, when the cabin door opened and Jackson emerged. David ducked back out of sight. Jackson carried a harness. He went to Keno and began fitting it on the dog. David kept the shed between them, backed away through the brush, and hurried off.

He met Grace on the corner, and the moment she got off the bus, he said, "You want to see Scrub? Come on."

They hurried up the trail, through the brush, and crept behind the shed. "Peek around the corner real easy," David whispered. "Don't let Jackson see you. Scrub's the first one."

Grace carefully inched her head out. "Gee!" she whispered back, "he's beautiful, just like you said. He looks exactly like that little carving we saw."

"You can go out and take a good look at him if you want," David said. "I can't. If Scrub sees me, he'll start barking; then Jackson will come out and there'll be trouble."

Grace stepped from behind the shed and approached Scrub. Scrub turned and faced her, big head down, amber eyes looking obliquely up at her as she approached. Then he lifted his head, and his tail began to wave. Grace was within a few feet of him, when the door opened and Jackson's nasal voice yelled, "Hey, kid, whatta you think you're doin'?"

"I—I'm looking at them," Grace stammered.

"What's a kid like you lookin' at dogs for?" Jackson demanded suspiciously.

She pointed at Scrub. "I've heard about him. That's Scrub, isn't it?"

"Where'd you hear about him?"

"In the paper. They said he was a great lead dog."

"Said that, huh?" Jackson was pleased. "All right, you can have a look."

Grace walked closer to Scrub. He stood at the end of his chain, waving his tail in invitation. "Can I pet him?" she asked.

"No. You've had a good look. Now beat it. Get!"

Grace ran back to David behind the shed, and they left hurriedly, keeping the shed between them and Jackson. Once down the trail Grace said, "I don't like that Smiley Jackson. He looks mean. I wish there was some way we could get Scrub away from him."

"There's no way," David said. "Besides, how could we keep him in the city? Aunt Margaret says no dogs."

130

"I know."

School closed. The next three days, Anchorage gave over to the Fur Rendezvous—"The Rondy," Alaskans called it. Holiday air gripped the city. Everything was done with but one thing in mind, entertainment and fun.

Trappers emerged from the wilderness with their winter harvests of furs. All along the street racks were set up and hung with furs where people might shop and bargain. A fur auction would be part of the festivities. There were stalls of Eskimo carvings and trinkets.

There would be games and contests of all kinds, a footrace in the snow, a parka parade, a children's one-dog race. A dignitaries' race would feature the mayor and two of the city's leading businessmen and the queen of the Fur Rendezvous. Two radio disc jockeys planned a race with the radio station operators.

A spectacle never before seen was scheduled this year. The queen and her court were to be pulled through the streets by teams of dogs hooked end-to-end almost a quarter-mile in length. Scramble races, in which drivers tried to snatch dollar bills from an overhead wire, a weight-pulling contest for single dogs, and a weight-carrying match for men were all part of the entertainment.

The big race for a five-thousand-dollar first prize was the event that claimed all Anchorage's attention. It was seventy-five miles and would be run in three heats of twenty-five miles each day. The team with the fastest overall time for the three days would be declared winner. The course wound across the tundra, through brush, timber, and ravines, making a twenty-five-mile circle that ended back at the starting line. Checkers stationed along the trail would make sure rules were obeyed. A helicopter would fly over the course, radioing the progress of the teams back to the crowd waiting in Anchorage.

Wherever people congregated, the talk was of mushers, teams, and lead dogs. David soon learned the names of the favorites and how the betting was going. Charlie White, an Eskimo from Kotzebue, was the choice to win. After that came Mel Johnson and Eddie Small, in that order. Other names cropped up to place, but no one topped Charlie White to win. David heard Jackson's name mentioned a number of times, but no one picked him to win or even to place in the money.

The morning the race began, most of Anchorage was present to see the start. Fourth Street was roped off to hold back the crowd and give teams and mushers room. David was there, with his uncle and aunt and Grace. Terry was off somewhere with his friends. The thirty teams were lined up waiting the starter's gun. Jackson had drawn number seventeen. He would start in that position. The teams would take off at two-minute intervals.

David moved up behind people and got to within a few feet of Scrub. Every dog knew what was to happen and was alert and anxious.

The team holding number one position pulled to the

132

starting line. The pistol cracked. The dogs went flying down the street to the cheers of the crowd. One by one the teams took off. When Jackson's turn came, David crowded close. At the sound of the pistol, the team lunged forward as one dog. Scrub led the team down the street at breakneck speed and out onto the tundra. A man near David said, "Nice start. That leader really takes 'em."

A few minutes later the helicopter began sending back information on the progress of the race. Radios along the street relayed the reports. Uncle George and Aunt Margaret wandered about among the racks of furs and Eskimo carvings. The children's one-dog race was about to begin. The parka parade would follow to fill in time until the teams began arriving back in town.

David and Grace hunted up a radio and listened to the helicopter reports. At the ten-mile mark Jackson passed number sixteen, then number fifteen. Other teams were passing, dropping back, passing again.

A half dozen had already been scratched for infractions of the rules. One team took out after a cow moose that crossed the trail in front of it. The dogs wrapped the sled around a tree. Two teams got into a fight, and both were so badly tangled they were eliminated. At the twenty-mile mark Jackson passed number fourteen.

David caught himself saying under his breath, "Come on, Scrub! Come on!" He was pulling for Smiley Jackson too, but he didn't care.

"Scrub's winning! He's winning!" Grace burst out.

"Not yet," David said, "but he's catching them."

The radio blared, "Jackson, number seventeen, passed thirteen. This Jackson team is coming!"

The children's race and the parka parade were over. The crowd began congregating again at the finish line.

"They'll start coming in a few minutes," David said. "Let's go watch them come into town."

They raced through an alley to the next street. The teams would come off the tundra here, turn and race down the main street to the finish line.

A small crowd had already gathered. They waited about ten minutes, then the first team came over the horizon. Other teams began appearing one by one. A big man near David watched through powerful binoculars and announced each team to the crowd as it appeared. "Charlie White, the Eskimo from Kotzebue, is leading. There comes Mel Johnson, in second place, and Eddie Small in third. The next three I don't know. That seventh one looks familiar." He screwed the eyepieces around. "It's Jackson! And look at that big leader dig in! He's gonna pass number six."

David's heart leaped. "Mister, would you let me look through those glasses?" he asked tensely.

The man glanced down, "They'll be here soon, boy."

"Smiley Jackson's lead dog belongs to Davie," Grace piped.

The man lowered the glasses and looked at David. Then he handed them to the boy. "Here, musher, watch your dog come in. He's a real go-getter."

David picked up Scrub immediately. The trail was

wide. There was plenty of room to pass. Scrub was even with the lead dog of number six position. His big head was down, his back humped. He was digging in for all he was worth.

Grace was yanking on David's sleeve, fairly dancing. "Let me see, Davie! Let me see!"

He handed her the glasses. She looked and began yelling, "He's passing! He's passed! He's in fifth!"

The big man said, "Good," and reached for the glasses.

A minute later the first five teams swept into the street. Jackson was holding down fifth place. He popped the whip over the dogs' straining backs and yelled like mad. They had passed so many teams on the trail that his time could make him winner of the race.

"Come on!" David grabbed Grace's hand and they ran back through the alley for the finish line to hear the time announced.

All five teams had crossed. Every dog was flat on the snow. Some were plainly exhausted. David's eyes found Scrub. He was lying down, but his big head was up, his tongue lolling out, panting. He was tired, but to David he looked as if he could go again.

Other teams were arriving amidst confusion and uproar. People shouted encouragement, dogs barked. A team ran wild into the crowd. For some strange reason, one team took a fancy to a light pole and began circling it at top speed to howls from the crowd and the angry shouts of the musher. Down the street a man with a camera stepped into the path of a running team and snapped its picture. At the flash the startled dogs jumped the curb onto the sidewalk, smashing the sled. A half-dozen spectators promptly tossed the cameraman head first into a snowbank.

David paid no attention. He was waiting for the public-address system to announce the time. The voice boomed over the crowd and stilled the noise. "Ladies and Gentlemen! Ladies and Gentlemen! In first place, Charlie White, time, two hours, thirty seconds. Second place, Smiley Jackson, time, two hours, three minutes, and fifty seconds. Third place, N.Y. Sullivan, two hours, five minutes, and ten seconds. Fourth, Wilfred Thompson, two hours, seven minutes, and forty-seven seconds."

David didn't wait for more. Scrub was second, only three minutes, twenty seconds behind first place. Maybe tomorrow he'd be first.

When David got into bed that night, he looked at the little ivory statue a long time. He kept seeing Scrub as he swung into the street head down, digging. The excitement of the race kept bubbling within him. He got very little sleep.

Only twenty-one teams started the second day. David and Grace watched the start and cheered when Scrub led his team down the street and out onto the tundra.

The dignitaries' race between the mayor, the businessmen, the Rendezvous Queen, and the grudge race between the disc jockeys occupied the time until the teams began returning. David and Grace stuck close to the radio to hear the helicopter reports.

The only team ahead of Jackson was Charlie White. He held his position, but Jackson was close on his heels. Behind them other teams jockeyed back and forth. Again David and Grace ran down the alley to the other street to watch the teams come in off the tundra.

The big man with the binoculars was there. He grinned at David and held out the glasses. "Hi, musher. Wanta watch your dog come in?"

Scrub was scant feet behind Charlie White when the team hit the end of the street. He held that spot all the way to the finish line. David and Grace dashed back down the alley to hear the time announced.

"Number one, Smiley Jackson, two hours, two minutes, seven seconds. Number two, Charlie White, two hours, five minutes, fifty-seven seconds." Scrub had a thirty-second lead in overall time.

When they reached home, David went immediately to his room. He wanted to be alone to think about the race and Scrub. He was happy the dog had won. The betting was changing. The talk on the street when he left favored Jackson to win the final heat. David was sure that after the final twenty-five-mile race tomorrow Scrub would be a champion. He wondered what the people of Aurora would think then about the scrub they'd rocked and chased all winter. He'd give anything to hold that big head in his hands again, to put his arms around the dog's neck, and press his face against the furry forehead.

Excitement was high the next morning when the starter's gun sent the teams pounding down the street. There were sixteen teams still in the race. They were soon gone.

The intervening time was taken up by the weight-pulling contest for single dogs, the scramble race, and the obstacle race. But this time David noticed more people clustered about the radios, following the progress of the race. At the ten-mile post two teams were scratched for rule infractions. A dog collapsed on number twenty-one, which meant that team would not do well. Number fifteen crashed into a rock and broke a sled runner. The first four teams to leave the starting line held their positions. Charlie White had closed a little on Jackson but not enough to try to pass.

At mile fifteen the positions of the first four remained unchanged. At mile twenty, number nineteen, in fifth place, moved up and closed on the fourth-place sled of Wilfred Thompson. Jackson still clung to first place, with Charlie White on his heels.

"Come on," David said, "let's see them come in."

Once again Grace and he raced hand in hand through the alley to the next street. The small crowd was there. The big man with the binoculars was scanning the trail. "Do you see them yet?" David asked breathlessly.

"Oh, hello, musher. No, not yet. But I heard your dog was still holding a slim lead."

A couple of minutes later the man said, "Here comes one. And there's another, and another."

138

"Who's leading?" David asked excitedly. "Is Scrub and Smiley Jackson leading?"

"Pretty far yet. Can't tell for sure." He screwed the eyepieces around. "Ah! there they are." He handed the glasses to David. "Here, see for yourself."

Scrub came into the lens in the lead. His head was down, his back hunched with effort. The whole team was running with every ounce of speed and strength they possessed. He could see Jackson on the handle bars, see his arm swing back and forward. It was too far to hear the crack of the lash. Charlie White was close behind Jackson, his dogs straining every ounce. The next three teams were coming into view, closely bunched.

Grace jerked at his sleeve, "Let me see, Davie. Let me see!" She had her look and began dancing up and down chanting, "Scrub's going to win! He's going to win."

"Maybe." The big man reached for his glasses. "But Charlie White's too close for comfort. Jackson could come in first but still lose the race, if White picks up the few seconds he lost yesterday. Remember, you win on the shortest overall time, young lady."

"I forgot," Grace said.

The team hit the end of the street. Jackson jumped from the runners and began to run, shoving the sled right up on the tail enders, so the dogs didn't have to pull even the light weight of the sled. All they had to do was run, and Scrub kept the line straight and headed down the center of the street. Behind them Charlie

White had jumped off the runners and was pushing.

"It's gonna be close," the big man said. "If Jackson can hold the pace, he's got it by a couple of seconds." He let out a wild yell, "Come on, Jackson! Come on, Scrub! Come on!" The rest of the crowd began to chant, "Come on, Scrub! Come on!"

David was so excited he didn't realize he'd moved a step beyond the rest and was shouting at the top of his voice, "Come on, Scrub! Come on! You can do it! Go! Go! Go!"

His voice, sharp, clear, and high carried to the sensitive ears of the dog. Scrub turned his head. The amber eyes searched the crowd and found the boy. With a glad bark, he headed straight for David. The whole team followed obediently. Jackson began to scream and curse. The whip lashed out again and again.

David suddenly realized what had happened. He yelled, "No, Scrub. No! No! Go back. Go back!" The sound of his voice only added to the dog's desire to reach him. David turned to run back into the crowd and lose himself. His foot struck a piece of ice and he sprawled in the snow. The next moment Scrub was on him whining and crying and licking his face. He tried to push the dog off, to get to his feet. Scrub kept whimpering and licking his face. His weight knocked David flat.

David was on his knees, trying to rise and fending off the ardent Scrub, when Smiley Jackson was upon them. He slashed at David's head with the heavy butt

140

of the whip. The blow knocked him down. Then he struck again and again at Scrub in an insane rage. His lips were drawn back, his face twisted. The long scar pulled the corners of his mouth into grotesque shape. He struck at David again. Remembering that other time, David threw his arms over his face and tried to roll away. The clubbing landed on his shoulders, head, and back with numbing force.

Then it was stopped. The big man had torn the whip from Jackson's hands. Others dragged him away.

David scrambled to his feet as the second-, third-, and fourth-place teams flashed past, heading for the finish line.

"I'll get you," Jackson kept screaming. "I'll get you. You done that on purpose."

A man held Scrub. He pulled and whined and whimpered, trying to get to David. Others turned the team around and led it up the street, out of David's sight. The big man handed Jackson his whip without a word. Jackson held the whip and glared at David. The presence of spectators kept him from leaping on the boy. He started to speak, then shook his head with a savage gesture, and turned away. He went to his team and headed it into a side street. He had not only lost first place, he was out of the money. And the fact that he had struck a spectator would surely disqualify him from the race.

Grace held David's arm and asked anxiously, "Gee, Davie, are you all right? He hit you awful hard."

141

His head ached. But his cap and turned-up collar had dulled most of the blow. "I'm all right," he muttered.

The big man said, "Your Scrub ran a mighty good race, musher. I'm sorry he lost."

- 11 -

Smiley Jackson was convinced an evil force had teamed up David and Scrub to make him lose the first prize, causing him to look like a fool in the eyes of the Anchorage citizens. Winning the Fur Rendezvous would have made him a musher to be reckoned with. That meant almost as much to Jackson as the prize money did. And now he might be barred from competing in the Fur Rendezvous forever for having struck a spectator.

There was nothing he could do about the boy, he thought savagely, as he took the team out of town. He would kill the dog when he reached the cabin.

It was a slow trip to the cabin, for the dogs were near exhaustion. There was time for his explosive temper to cool and his devious mind to begin thinking of ways to overcome this loss. His naturally greedy nature and gambling instincts began to assert themselves. There would be another race soon, the North American in Fairbanks. The cash prize was almost as large as this one. The honor of winning was great. But he needed a good lead dog. A team is only as good as its leader.

He had to admit Scrub had done a good job leading the team for all but the last minute of the last day. He'd had the race won. The same mushers would be at Fairbanks for the North American. He'd really won over them here. He could win at Fairbanks. Much as he hated the thought, he needed Scrub to do the job. After he won, Scrub could be sold for a good price or traded for another strong leader. But one thing Jackson promised himself, he'd not keep Scrub beyond the Fairbanks race, for someday he'd surely lose his temper and kill the dog.

Jackson was almost broke. Most of the money he'd won at the smaller races had gone for expenses. If he could make Fairbanks, he'd have to look for another sponsor to help with his entrance fee and the care of the dogs. If he won the Fairbanks North American, he'd be financially set up for the coming year. He'd win it, Jackson told himself grimly, if he had to run Scrub to death doing it.

Jackson stayed around Anchorage for the remainder of the Fur Rendezvous celebration. It was an exciting time, and there was no telling what sort of opportunity might present itself. A couple of men came up and looked at the dogs. One asked if the team was for sale.

Jackson thought quickly, sizing up the man, and said, "Six thousand."

"You're crazy," the man said.

"This team almost won the Rondy," Jackson pointed

144

out. "But for an accident, I would have. I'm gonna win the North American next month."

"Maybe," the man said.

"Come watch me," Jackson challenged.

"I might do that," the man said and left.

The day after the celebration ended, Jackson hitched up the team and headed for Fairbanks. It was more than three hundred miles. The trip took the better part of a week.

There are always old vacant cabins on the outskirts of northern towns. Jackson found one at Fairbanks, staked out the dogs, and moved in with his sleeping bag.

Already Fairbanks was in a festive mood. Many of the mushers who had participated in the Fur Rendezvous were here for the North American. Every day they ran their teams out across the tundra, keeping the dogs in shape for the grueling race they knew the North American to be.

Jackson hadn't time to work his dogs. He had to spend his days visiting business people in search of a sponsor who'd help with expenses. A week convinced him that the big backers of racing teams were already pledged. Others who might like to could not afford it.

A racing team is expensive to keep and Jackson's thin bankroll was soon gone. He had money to feed himself and the dogs another week. The race was almost two weeks away. By then he wouldn't have even the entry fee. There were two things left he could do, sell the team here or take it back to Aurora. If he returned to Aurora, he'd have to work to support the dogs until next winter's racing season.

The thought of any kind of work was distasteful to Jackson. Maybe he could sell the dogs for a good price and turn a nice profit. The thought of selling the team didn't bother him. He'd done it before.

Jackson went about among the mushers, to the bars, wherever people gathered to talk dog racing. He dropped the word that his team was for sale. Then he waited.

Several people came and looked at the team. None were interested enough to ask his price or make an offer. He waited until he'd used up most of the dog food. Then he knew he had to return to Aurora.

The night before Jackson planned to leave, a man came to look at the team. Philip Hansen was short and stocky. He looked trail-hard. The way he sized up each dog, Jackson guessed he knew what he was about. "Heard you want to sell your team," he said.

"If I get my price."

"Saw 'em perform in Anchorage," Hansen said. "You should have won that race."

"I almost did."

Hansen was looking at Scrub. "What's your price?"

"You figurin' to race 'em?"

"Possibly. How much?"

Jackson thought swiftly. "Five thousand."

"I'll give you four. I don't want this one."

"He's a good leader," Jackson said.

146

"He wasn't that last day in Anchorage."

"That was an accident. He saw somebody he knew and liked. It could happen to any dog."

"I still don't want him. Four thousand for the rest of the team. You ought to be able to peddle your leader to somebody. That'd bring you out close to the five you're asking."

Jackson knew it was take this or return broke to Aurora and work all year to support the dogs. Four thousand was more than he'd ever had at one time. And, as Hansen said, he could probably sell Scrub. Leaders were always in demand. With four thousand he could buy a team for next winter and have money left over. "All right," he said, "it's a deal."

Hansen took out his wallet and extracted bills. "I can't take the team now. I've got to go on north. I'll give you a thousand and the rest when I get back in two weeks. I'll pay for the care of the dogs while I'm gone."

"Two weeks, you say?"

"You don't want to wait?" Hansen asked.

"It's not that," Jackson's thoughts were racing. Here was the money for his entrance fee and the North American would be run next week. "Long's your gonna be gone," he said casually, "I might as well enter them in the race."

"They haven't had a workout in two weeks," Hansen said. "They wouldn't stand a chance."

"I think they would."

"No," Hansen's voice was flat. "No team of mine runs unless it's in top condition and has a chance to win. This one hasn't."

Jackson started to argue, then changed his mind. "Whatever you say."

"Good. Let's get a piece of paper and make this legal. I'll see you in two weeks."

Excitement for the North American began to build. Jackson moved among the teams, studying the dogs, talking to mushers. He watched their daily workouts and became attracted to one. Dusty Summers' team was young and eager. It was led by an older dog that was smart, unexcitable, and steady. Jackson was sure they had a good chance, if not to win at least to place. The odds were great against their winning, and three to one that they would not place in the money. Here was an opportunity to recoup some of the prize money he'd lost at the Fur Rendezvous. But he'd play it safe. He bet the thousand dollars Hansen had given him on Dusty Summers' team to place. The three he could win, added to the four thousand he'd got for the team, would give him seven thousand dollars. With such an amount he could buy the best-trained team in the country and sweep the North American and the Fur Rendezvous next winter.

Dusty Summers drew number ten for the race, and Jackson was at the starting line to see him off. There were a couple of accidents, and a half-dozen teams were scratched for rule infractions within the first fifteen miles. As at Anchorage, Charlie White was first to cross the finish line. Behind him came N. Y. Sullivan in second, and a new man Jackson had never heard of, Ned Clark, in third. Dusty Summers was fourth, fifteen seconds behind the leader. The second day Summers passed Clark and came in third. He had picked up five seconds. He was ten seconds behind the leader in overall time. Jackson's hopes were high.

The final day, Jackson watched them go flying out of town, then hunted up a radio to get the reports from the trail. At the ten-mile spot Summers was holding well to third place. At fifteen he began closing on the number two team, N. Y. Sullivan. Summers passed Sullivan at the twenty-mile checkpoint and was running strongly in number two position. Then a mile later and within minutes of the finish, tragedy struck. Summers' old lead went lame. He got the dog out of harness and into the basket and put one of the other dogs in as leader. But it was no longer the same team. The dogs' speed and drive were gone. Sullivan passed them, then Ned Clark. Other teams overtook them. Summers came into town running ninth, completely out of the money.

Hours later Jackson found Summers and a half-dozen other mushers who'd lost congregated in a bar, morosely explaining their losses over drinks. Jackson joined them.

"My team wasn't used to crowds," Dave Wright said. "All that hollerin' and yellin' bothered 'em."

"Noise didn't bother my dogs," Marshall said. "They just wasn't in condition for this tough a grind."

A third insisted the trail was soft and that the teams

ahead of him had chewed it up, so that he slid around.

"I thought I had her made," Summers said. "Number two in the North American and my first race." He shook his head sadly. "I was already livin' it up, when, bam! Hobo goes lame."

"He's too old," Jackson said. "You should have retired him at least a year ago."

"I thought he could make it. He's been a mighty good dog."

"With a young leader like mine, you'd have been in the big money. I'll sell you Scrub reasonable. He's young and strong. I've got no more use for 'im."

"I've got a young dog at home I'll use next season," Summers said.

"Mine's already trained," Jackson pointed out. "He almost took the Fur Rendezvous."

"I couldn't buy him if I wanted to," Summers confessed. "I've spent all my spare cash."

Jackson approached the others around the table. None wanted a lead dog.

Jackson returned to the cabin. One way or the other he told himself, he meant to get rid of Scrub before he left Fairbanks.

The racing season was over. The mushers disappeared, and Fairbanks settled back to normal. Jackson stayed on, waiting for Hansen to return for his dogs. He was running short of dog feed, so he cut down a little. He cut Scrub's rations in half.

Hansen finally returned, paid Jackson the remaining

three thousand dollars, and took the dogs. Scrub was all Jackson had left.

Now that he had money, Jackson decided to stay a few more days to try to sell Scrub. Mushers, prospectors, and trappers frequented a certain bar. Jackson went there. The bar also had a number of card tables.

Jackson was an inveterate gambler and eventually sat in a game. He won a hundred dollars. The next day he won again. Maybe, he decided, as long as he was on a run of good luck, he could win not only the money he hoped to get for Scrub but the thousand he'd lost betting on the race. At a thousand, he told himself, he'd quit.

At first Jackson won steadily. Then he lost—and won again. At the end of three days he'd won five hundred dollars. But he never reached the magic one thousand. Gradually he began to lose. But he couldn't quit. The fever was upon him. His luck would change. He had to win back his losses.

He paid little attention to Scrub. The dog went for days without food, sometimes even without a drink. His exercise was limited to the few feet of chain. His coat became dull gray.

A woman who passed every day finally brought him water and a plate of scraps from her own table.

The first breath of an early spring blew across the land. The snow turned to slush. Patches of green and yellow tundra began to appear. Winter's back was broken. Jackson was still gambling and losing steadily now. He was down to his last eight hundred dollars, when he had cause to think of Scrub again.

He was in the bar one night, sitting at a table with a half-dozen other men, among them a musher named Harvey James. James had been bragging how good his lead dog, Old Bob was. Jackson was in an ugly mood. Yesterday he'd won a sizable amount and was sure he was on his way back. Tonight he was losing again.

"Old Bob saved my life last year," James said. "Went through rotten ice, me and the sled and the whole team right up to Old Bob. Didn't get him though. No, siree. Know what he done? That dog just stiffened his back and dug in his claws right at the edge of the hole and pulled me, the sled, and the whole team right out again. Musta been close to an eight-hundred-pound pull."

"Call that a pull?" Jackson asked scornfully.

"Yeah," James bridled, "I do."

"Scrub 'ud take that without even breathin' hard."

"On slick ice?"

"Ice, pavement, snow, or plain old tundra, Scrub could pull your dog in two," Jackson bragged.

James looked around the table. "You hear that? And he even calls that mutt Scrub. You never saw the day he could outpull Old Bob."

"Easy to prove," the bartender sensed excitement. "Let 'em have a pulling match. There's still a patch of ice on the street in the shade of that new building a couple blocks up."

"I got a sled we can use," one man offered. "And a hundred dollars that says Scrub outpulls Bob."

152

A man across the table planked down bills, "And here's another hundred says he can't."

James held up a fistful of money and looked at Jackson. "All I got, five hundred, says Bob outpulls your dog."

Jackson thought of Scrub, young, big, and powerful. He'd seen Old Bob. His muzzle was gray. An old dog far past his prime. No dog that age could match the young, tough, Scrub. He brought out his thin roll of bills and counted off five hundred dollars.

Jackson and Harvey James went to get their dogs. The bar emptied. Everyone headed for the new building.

When Jackson arrived with Scrub, half a hundred men were there. The sled was loaded with concrete blocks, and Old Bob was hitched to it, waiting. A line had been drawn in the street some distance from the sled.

The bartender said, "There'll be no breakin' out the the sled. This'll be a straight pull. Each dog pulls the sled to that line. We've got eighteen blocks on here. I figure that's close to eight hundred pounds. We'll keep addin' blocks until one dog can't pull it. Harvey's ready to go."

Old Bob was as big as Scrub, with a broad chest and heavy legs. He stood quiet, looking about, waiting. He'd been through this before. He knew what was expected of him. James stepped in front of him and the dog's ears came forward. "All right," the man said quietly, "whenever you're ready take it away, Bob. Hike!"

153

Bob pulled experimentally, as if testing the load. Then he lunged into it. The runners creaked and moved. He hit straight ahead following Harvey James, who backed toward the finish line, bent over, holding out a hand, coaxing the dog quietly with his voice. "You can do it, boy. It's all yours. There! You've got it! That's it. Bring it along! Good boy."

The sled gathered momentum under Old Bob's flying feet. When he crossed the finish line, the sled was almost coasting.

The sled was pulled back to the starting line, Bob was taken out, and Jackson buckled Scrub into the harness. Jackson had his whip, and Harvey said, "No strikin' the dog."

"Nothin' was said about what I might hafta do to make 'im pull."

"That's right," the bartender agreed. "Just so he pulls it."

This was new to Scrub. He knew he was supposed to do something. But he'd always had the team behind him before. Then Jackson's voice said sharply, "All right, Scrub. Let's go. Hike! Hike!"

Scrub lunged forward but was brought up short. The sled did not start easily. Jackson's voice shouted, "Come on! Hike! Hike!" Scrub humped his back. His claws dug grooves in the street ice. The load moved sluggishly, moved again. It kept moving and was still picking up speed when Scrub crossed the finish line.

Four more blocks were added, and Bob was harnessed to the sled. He fell on his first attempt. On the second lunge, he got the sled moving and kept it going to cross the line. But it was obvious he wasn't going to pull much more.

Scrub had learned from the first pull. Now he hunched his big body and lunged into the harness, feet flying. The load started, but he picked up no speed and the finish line crept forward with agonizing slowness. He was shaking when Jackson stopped him. In the days he'd lain idle and less than half-fed he'd lost weight and his muscles had become soft and flabby. Every man there knew he was pulling on heart alone.

This time they added two blocks. Bob had trouble starting it. But he was in fine condition for an old dog. He got it going, and kept it moving with agonizing slowness all the way to the line, where he collapsed. He had pulled his limit.

The sled was hauled back and once again Scrub was harnessed to it. The muscles of his legs still quivered from his last effort and his big chest could not get enough air. At Jackson's command he lunged to the job. He fell, but was up instantly, feet digging, his body bunched compactly. The crowd watched in silence knowing what the effort was costing him. They could hear the breath rasp in his throat, his toe nails tearing at the ice. The load moved! It kept moving! Scrub's head was down, his chest low to the ice with his tremendous effort. The sympathy of everyone went out to the gallant dog, for by now they all knew Smiley Jackson. Even Harvey James had forgotten what this win would mean to him in admiration for Scrub's last-ounce try. Ten feet! Twenty feet! A man let out a relieved yell that was picked up by half a hundred throats.

Then Scrub collapsed. The sled stopped.

Smiley Jackson shouted, "Get up! Get up! Hike! Hike!"

Scrub got shakily to his feet. He lunged into the load, but there was only his weight and fierce desire. There was no strength behind the effort. He fell and lay there.

Jackson rushed at him like a madman. He smashed his foot into the dog's quivering body screaming, "Get up! Get up. Hike! Hike!" He brought the butt of the whip down on the dog's back again and again.

Scrub felt the pain and tried to rise. But for the moment he could not.

The bartender leaped on Jackson and tore the whip from his hands. A couple of men pinned Jackson's arms and dragged him away from the prostrate dog. Harvey James unhitched Scrub and gently got him on his feet.

"It's not the dog's fault," the bartender said angrily to Jackson. "If he wasn't half-starved and out of condition, he'd have pulled that load. Take your dog and get out of here."

Jackson held out his hand, "I'll take my whip."

The bartender shook his head. "You're too handy with it. I'll just keep it. If you ever show your face around my bar again, I'll use it on you. Now get moving."

Someone handed Jackson Scrub's chain, and he went down the street dragging the dog with him. Once again

156

Scrub had betrayed him. His rage at the dog was building with every step, but he dared do nothing within sight of that crowd. He turned a corner and was out of sight. He stopped abruptly, jerked the dog toward him, and aimed a tremendous kick at his head. The kick missed. Jackson's feet flew from under him, and he fell flat on his back.

Scrub dodged back at the kick and, in doing so, jerked the chain from Jackson's slackened grip. He backed away as the man scrambled to hands and knees. Jackson reached for the end of the chain. "Whoa," he said. "Whoa." At that command Scrub stopped obediently. All Jackson had to do was step forward and pick up the chain. But his anger at the dog was all-consuming. A club lay close at hand. He grabbed it and surged to his feet, bent on crushing the dog's skull.

Scrub knew what the club meant. He whirled and ran off down the street glancing back over his shoulder. Jackson hurled the club. Scrub dodged, and it sailed harmlessly past. The dog ran straight on to the end of the street and out onto the dark tundra, the loose chain dragging behind.

Jackson watched the dog disappear, then turned, and headed for the cabin. He was practically broke. He'd lost the dog he'd stayed in Fairbanks to sell. There was nothing to keep him here now. He'd have to go back to Aurora.

He thought of Scrub running across the tundra dragging the chain. The dog wouldn't get far before he hung up on some obstruction. It was very possible he might find the dog when the chain became tangled in a bush or around a log. If I do, Jackson thought savagely, I'll kill him immediately. Should have done it long ago. Scrub was bad luck, a hoodoo from the day he was born.

At the cabin Jackson began getting ready to leave the next morning. He had the odd feeling that he hadn't seen the last of Scrub. Somewhere out there on the tundra the dog and he would come face to face again.

- 12 -

Scrub fled blindly across the dark tundra. He was free
for the first time in months, and he meant to get as far
from Smiley Jackson as possible. The chain around his
neck was an immediate problem. He ran with his head
turned sideways to avoid tripping over it. It was constantly snagging on grass clumps, a bush, or rock, and
jerking on his neck. Once the end wrapped about a
bush and brought him up short. He circled the bush
pulling at it. Luckily he unwound the chain and was
free again. He soon learned to skirt brush clumps, to
steer clear of rocks, and managed to avoid many hold-
ups.

Scrub ran until he was exhausted and had to lie
down. The snow was mostly gone, and the tundra was
damp and cold. After a few minutes' rest, he sat up and
looked about. Fairbanks was not even a light fan in
the night sky. All about him the dark shape of the
tundra stretched away broken only by black brush
patches, and the thin silhouettes of trees thrust against
a pale skyline. There was not a whisper of sound. A

breeze blew softly out of the south. He thrust his nose into the tundra moss and sniffed loudly, filling his nostrils with the pungent scent of the earth and the first taint of returning spring. He still had the chain about his neck, but now it was not attached to a stake. He was free to go where he liked. He stood, turning his head, as though getting his bearings. Then he set off at a steady trot, going due south, dragging the chain behind him. He was heading for the one person he loved. He was going home to Aurora, home to the boy.

Scrub traveled all night, with frequent stops to rest. The dragging chain slowed him up. By great good luck he passed safely through the belt of trees and brush without becoming firmly caught and came to a section of flat, barren tundra where there was little to snag the chain. He was ravenously hungry and thirsty. But there was neither game nor streams on this flat expanse.

Morning found Scrub miles away, entering an area of low rolling hills that grew a scattering of brush and trees. Numerous small streams wandered across the land. Most were already ice free.

Scrub drank from the first stream, then lay on the bank to rest. The water stilled his hunger pangs for the moment. His keen ears picked up the high voices of geese heading north. He tilted his head but could not see them. A flight of ducks fled over, following the course of the stream. They were so low the missile-like whistling of their passage made him duck. A sixth sense told him he had entered an area that should contain game. But he saw none.

160

He traveled again, careful to avoid brush and trees that could snag the chain. The hunger pangs returned. He was constantly on the lookout for food.

The warming sun brought forth a mouse and a shrew. Scrub caught both. But they were mere bites. A ptarmigan hen exploded out of the dead grass at his feet. His leap to knock it down fell short when the chain caught momentarily on a grass clump.

An hour later he ran into luck when he stumbled into a colony of ground squirrels on a sunny hillside. They chattered shrilly and scattered, diving headfirst into holes. One was a second too slow, and Scrub's big jaws snapped shut on its back. Afterward he lay in the sun resting. The curious squirrels emerged to investigate. He caught another.

When he resumed traveling, his hunger was satisfied.

The chain was forever snagging on something and yanking on his neck. He moved slowly and traveled far out of his way to find smooth going. Even so, his neck became sore from the continued jerking. Links along the chain and the big ring in the end became plugged with dead grass and weeds making it a heavy drag. This acted as a constant reminder that kept him on guard.

He found no more food and spent the night curled up in a hollow at the base of a rock. He awoke hungry, his neck stiff and sore from the chafing and tugging of the dragging chain. He drank at a small stream and headed toward a great jumble of blue and white mountains. He rested often. The drag on the chain seemed to have increased and was sapping his strength. It was wearing a raw spot around his neck.

An hour's travel brought him to a stream too large to jump and too deep to wade. He drank from the edge, then looked at the far bank. Across that water was the way to go. The current was swift. Big chunks of ice kept shooting past. Breakup had been just hours before. He waited for a clear spot of water, then waded in and struck out for the opposite shore. The chain dragged along the rocky bottom and slowed him down. He was over halfway, when the chain snagged on something and stopped him. He paddled furiously to pull loose but could not. He was held fast. Water boiled over his back. His head went under.

A big block of ice boomed down the current and struck the chain. The block slid along and slammed into the dog. It drove him deep and tore at him. Then it was gone. He struggled to the surface still paddling toward the far shore. His feet struck bottom, and he staggered up the bank and collapsed.

Scrub lay a long time getting back his strength and vomiting water. Finally he got weakly to his feet and went slowly up the valley. The chain pulled easier. The swift water and the rubbing ice cake had washed out much of the dry grass and twigs that had collected in the links.

He had to have food, and game was plentiful in the valley. There were ptarmigans, grouse, squirrels, and rabbits in abundance. But the chain kept him from catching them. As he approached the mountains and

162

the valley narrowed down, it became rougher. It was only a matter of time before the chain would hang up.

He didn't know where the rabbit came from, but suddenly it was running almost under his nose. He leaped after it. The rabbit dived into a hole in a rock pile. The hole was shallow. Scrub could see the rabbit crouched back in the dark. Its scent was strong, and saliva dripped from Scrub's jaws. He tried to enlarge the hole to admit his head. But his claws hit rock. He spent a half hour trying to get at the rabbit, then gave up. He turned to leave and was brought up short by the chain. The ring on the end had slipped between two rocks and was wedged fast. He pulled just hard enough to convince himself he was securely held, then he calmly lay down. In his mind he was fastened as securely as if he was again staked out in front of Smiley Jackson's cabin.

He was lying in the sun and soon became thirsty. Hunger pangs kept his eyes glued to the hole where food was so close. He closed his eyes and appeared to nap. But every few minutes he opened them and stared into the hole. His only movement was the slight lift of his sides as he breathed. Finally, the rabbit moved to the edge of the burrow and sat there. After a few more minutes it ventured timidly forth. Scrub lay perfectly still.

The rabbit, too, was hungry and there were tender new grass shoots a few feet away. It hopped to the first and ate them. It went to the next, and the next.

Scrub's powerful back legs were curled under him.

163

His body tensed for the spring. The rabbit reached the next grass clump and began to eat. The dog launched himself through the air with all the strength he possessed. The rabbit dived for the hole.

Scrub's teeth were within an inch of clamping down on the rabbit's back when the chain tightened and sent him somersaulting among the rocks. He lay a moment, the wind knocked out of him. Then he got shakily to his feet and looked about. The rabbit was back in the hole. Scrub sniffed hopefully at the entrance and scratched experimentally at the rock. Then he trotted down off the rock pile.

At that moment he realized he was free of the hated chain. His savage lunge had been more than the rusty old links could take. It had broken within six inches of his neck. This short, dangling end would not hinder him. He trotted off through the brush, heading south.

Within an hour Scrub caught a ptarmigan that was scratching about in the brush. Later he raced a ground squirrel to a hole and caught it. That night he slept well-fed, curled between two huge rocks the sun had warmed during the day.

The following day the valley pinched down to a narrow ravine that led Scrub into the mountains. Here he could not follow the straight line that he had set for himself on the flat or rolling tundra. Sheer rock-battlements, deep, musty canyons, and towering mountains forced him to detour many miles. But this didn't confuse the dog. He knew the direction to go. Scrub

164

was following the homing instinct that has been part of the wild since time began.

The next couple of days took Scrub deep into the mountain range. He ate well now. Wildlife was abundant. Every open spot of water was crowded with birds. Rabbits and squirrels were everywhere. Porcupines hardly bothered to get out of his way. High on the crags, marmots whistled to warn other animals of his presence. Scrub didn't bother to look up. A ragged-looking grizzly not long out of winter sleep received the dog's careful attention.

Eventually Scrub came into an area of many streams. The ice was already gone from the smaller ones, and these he waded or swam. It was beginning to break up in some of the larger streams. These he'd hit at breakneck speed and race across so swiftly that he had no trouble.

So he came into land he remembered and found the big river. He didn't know he was traveling parallel to the trap line he'd been over with the boy. He only knew this was familiar.

When not frozen, the river was wide, deep, and swift. Now it lay, a twisting glare of ice caught between low banks. The ice of a hundred small streams was jammed against it, waiting for release and adding to the pressure. It was a long way across.

Scrub heard water running beneath the ice. On his side, a good-sized stream flowed between the bank and the main sheet of ice. The moving water cut steadily into the ice, loosening it. A series of sharp explosions sounded down-river. They were repeated up-river. The water running along the bank bothered him.

He looked at the far bank. He had to cross to continue his way.

With a running leap he shot over the water and sprawled on the ice. When he scrambled to his feet, Scrub discovered a film of water an inch deep flowing across the top of the ice. It made standing next to impossible. He began inching his way. The snapping and cracking in the distance grew louder. The ice trembled and moved beneath him.

Scrub tried to hurry. His feet flew from under him and he skidded on his side. He could travel only at a certain slow speed. He was halfway across, when the snapping and cracking was suddenly all about him. An inch-wide crack opened under his nose and snaked out ahead. Water bubbled up through the crack. Then cracks were fanning out in all directions. Pressure beneath sent water spurting into the air.

In fear Scrub tried to run. He fell and skidded through the spouting water. When he gained his feet, the whole river of ice was moving beneath him. It heaved, twisted, and broke with a mighty crash. Thunder was all about him. The great sheet of ice that had blanketed the river was breaking up.

Scrub found himself lying flat on a huge ice cake, his claws gripping frantically. He was being swirled wildly down the icy current that was surging in a boiling froth toward a distant sea.

166

Scrub fought to ride the slippery ice cake, but his claws couldn't hold. The cake pitched and tossed. It finally upended, throwing him into the racing torrent. He fought his way to the surface and struck out for the far bank, head outstretched, four feet driving. His amber eyes were fixed unwaveringly on his goal, the distant shore. Even here, in this cataclysm of smashing ice and raging water, with death waiting all about him, Scrub did not lose his sense of direction or the driving will to go on.

He was like a small chip tossed into a millrace. The current whipped him along, turning and twisting. It sucked him under and tumbled him about. The last moment, it tossed him carelessly to the surface. He was in a small, calm triangle formed by three big blocks wedged together. He tried to climb onto a block. He got his front paws over the edge and could go no further. There he hung, straining, while the current plunged him forward at express speed. All about him huge blocks smashed together with grinding force, or heaved on end to topple with shattering explosions that showered him with ice particles.

The ice block to which he clung tilted sharply downward and he slipped back into the water, clawing frantically. He was sucked under again. The three blocks broke apart and the triangle of calm water was gone.

Scrub surfaced some distance downstream. Small, speeding chunks of ice slammed into him like driven spears, but he continued swimming. The opposite bank approached with agonizing slowness.

But he could not go on forever. The battering he'd received was taking its toll. He was near the bank when his great heart gave out. His strength was gone, and though land was but a few feet off, he could not reach it. He continued stroking feebly, but he barely kept his nose above water. He was still stroking when he finally went under. A great slab of ice rose out of the tortured depths and smashed down above him.

When Scrub regained consciousness, he was lying on a rug on a floor. A fire was crackling merrily in a stove and delicious warmth was soaking into his battered body. A man with a steel hook was sitting on a bench and looking at him.

When he spoke, the dog's sharp ears came forward. He remembered the voice. "Well, friend," Scotty said, "I never expected to run into you again, much less fish you out of the breakup. Seems like savin' your life is getting to be a habit of mine. I had some doubts you'd wake up when I first brought you in. That old river almost got you for sure. But I remember you always was a tough one."

Scrub thumped his tail weakly on the floor, but he didn't try to move.

"That's right, rest," Scotty said. "You've earned it. You gave that old river as good a battle as I've ever seen. You'd of lost, though, but for me. Me and my hook." He held up his left arm. "For once it came in handy. I doubt I could of held onto you with a hand in that current. Once I got the hook in that chain there was no pullin' loose." He frowned and asked, "Where'd you leave Smiley Jackson? At the bottom of the river maybe? Well, he won't be greatly mourned."

Scotty was lonesome for talk. Even though his audience was only a dog, it was better than nothing. "I was watchin' the breakup and I saw you comin' for a couple hundred yards. Thought you was a wolf till you got close and the sun shone on that chain around your neck. Then I knew you had to be a dog. I ran down and waded out and snagged you. Didn't know it was you, though, till I hauled you out." He leaned forward and stroked Scrub's big head. "I'm right glad to see you, friend.

"You and me," he continued, "we're special. Know why? That old river got me once just like it did you. About twenty years ago, that was. Done the same thing you did, started across during breakup. I lost my team and sled and ever'thing. I got out alone though. I've seen a lotta animals get caught in the breakup along here—deer, moose, wolves, foxes, caribou. You and me, we're the only ones got caught in it and lived, friend. I guess, in a manner of speakin', that makes us brothers of some kind."

Scrub thumped his tail again, and Scotty continued, "You ain't bunged up too bad, considering you got some pretty good bangs from ice chunks. I'd guess you might have a cracked rib or two, but they'll heal in a few days. Mostly you're just bruised, same as I was. About tomorrow every muscle you got will start screamin' when you move. You'll be that sore."

169

Scotty rose. "I'll bet you're hungry. You've had a big day. You've come back and you lived through the breakup. I'd say that calls for a celebration and somethin' special, like maybe bacon pancakes. How's that sound to you? I'll bet you ain't had one since the last time you was here."

Scrub pounded his tail again, and Scotty nodded. "Bacon pancakes it is. You know, they really stick to your ribs. That's what you need a lot of now."

Scrub basked in the warmth of the room and listened to the rattle of pots and pans. Finally the delicious odors of cooking brought him to a sitting position, licking his lips.

When Scotty put a pan heaped with potatoes and pancakes before him, the dog dropped his head and dug in. Scotty sat at the table with his own loaded plate and smiled. "That's the stuff, friend," he said. "I like to see a guest enjoy his food."

Scrub licked the pan clean and lay back with a gusty sigh.

"You figure that'll hold you till morning?" Scotty asked. He poised a bite of pancake on his fork and said thoughtfully, "The way I figure it, you didn't leave Jackson in the river. That busted chain says you're alone, friend. Maybe Jackson sold you, maybe he didn't. But you broke loose from some place and you're headed back to Aurora because you think Davie's there. I hate to disappoint you, but he's gone and never comin' back. There's nothing here for him to come back to. He's with his uncle now. Once that boy gets a taste of city life he'll never return to the bush. So what happens to you? I've got to think on that."

Later when he was getting ready for bed, Scotty said to the dog, "Don't remember if I told you I was glad to see you again, but I am. Sort of like having a bit of Davie and his folks again."

Scrub spent the night on the rug before the warm stove. In the morning he found that every muscle had stiffened and he could barely stand.

"Like I told you, eh?" Scotty said. "You found you got muscles you didn't know you had. It won't last long. In a couple of days you'll limber up. Just lay back, relax, and take life easy."

Scrub spent the day on the rug, rising stiffly only when Scotty set pans of food before him. Scotty put in the day working over the pile of furs David and his father caught during the winter. "The fur buyer'll be out in about a week and I want everything to look shipshape," he explained to Scrub. "After that I've got to repair my sluice boxes and do a little prospecting."

Later that evening Scotty said, "Been giving your case a lotta thought. The thing is, did you run off from Jackson or somebody else? If it was somebody else, he likely wouldn't know where to look for you. Now Jackson might come this way lookin' for you. I don't want him around here any time for any reason. Guess I've got a little more thinkin' to do."

Again Scrub spent the night on the rug before the stove. The next morning when he rose to eat, some of the stiffness was gone.

After breakfast Scrub limped outside. He looked toward the river. It was flowing smooth and free of ice. But great chunks lay melting along the bank where they'd been pushed by the breakup. He lifted his nose to the warm breeze as though reading some message it carried. Satisfied, he stretched out on his side and let the warm morning sun soak into him.

Scotty smiled from the open door. "In two or three days you'll be as good as new, friend, so don't be in a rush to go ramming around. You lay there and soak up that sun. Best medicine in the world." Scotty went back inside and through the open door the dog heard him moving about.

Scrub lay in the sun for some time. Then his head rose and turned toward the south. His sharp ears came forward. Finally he got stiffly to his feet.

Scotty's voice drifted to him from inside the cabin. "Finished my thinkin' about you, friend. Way I figure it is this: someplace you've got an owner. Whether he'll ever find you or not nobody knows. Right now you're a lost dog. You're heading back to Davie and he's not there. You're going to be mighty lonesome when you learn that. Now me, I didn't want another dog, but with Davie gone and his folks all gone it sure gets lonesome for somebody to talk to. That puts you and me in the same boat. You've got to forget Davie and stay with me. We can make a pretty good team of it. . . ."

Scrub moved slowly off through the trees. Scotty's voice faded into silence.

172

Scrub could not travel fast and the first few hours he stopped often to rest. But gradually, stiff, bruised muscles began limbering up. By late afternoon he was trotting along, relatively free of pain. He made no more stops to rest.

It was early evening, the sun was dropping behind the trees when he came to the spot on the river bank where David and he had fished and learned to walk again. When he entered the clearing and saw the cabin, he broke into a headlong run, barking wildly. He dashed up to the closed door and scratched and barked to be let in. He alternately scratched and barked for several minutes. Then he put his nose to the crack at the bottom of the door and sniffed. There was no smell of warmth from within, of cooking, or of any life.

He circled the cabin, looking for someone. He nosed about the half-used woodpile and the ground around the cabin searching for scent. But the winter snow and time had washed it all away. He visited the barren spots where the doghouses had stood. There was nothing. He reared against one of the windows and tried to peer inside, but the curtains were drawn. No sounds came to his straining ears. There was something he could not understand. He had lived with the boy in this house. Here he had known love and affection and family warmth. Now there was an air of desertion about the place and he could find no trace that anyone had ever been here.

He lay down on the porch, his back against the door, to wait. The boy would come.

Light faded out of the sky and darkness folded over the earth. The stars came out. The moon sailed from behind the distant peaks and bathed the clearing and cabin in soft light. In the distance ducks and geese talked companionably on the river. A rabbit darted across the clearing, pursued by a weasel. An owl called from the edge of timber and was answered from a long way off.

Morning brought no one. Scrub stayed close all day, intermittently napping on the porch and wandering about the clearing. His sharp ears were attuned for the slightest noise from within. His delicate nose kept searching for some remembered scent. Once he went to the river for a drink. He stood on the high bank and looked about. Memories stirred faintly within him. Finally he trotted back to the cabin. He scratched at the door at intervals and barked inquiringly. With evening he became very hungry. He trotted off toward Aurora.

His actions at the settlement were the same as when he was a starving pup. He visited the garbage piles first, but some other animal had picked them clean. He sneaked among the houses, his nose sampling the slight breeze for any scent of food. At the last house he found a hot dish sitting on a porch bench to cool. He slipped up on the porch, reared front paws on the bench and began bolting the contents of the dish. He was not as cautious as he had been as a pup. He rattled the pan and knocked it from the bench. Steps came toward the door. Scrub whirled and dashed off the

174

porch into the cover of night. A voice yelled angrily, "Get outa here! Beat it!"

A woman's voice called, "What'd you see, Harry?"

"Couldn't be sure in the dark," a man answered. "Dog of some kind, I think. He got most of your pie. If I didn't know Smiley Jackson was gone, I'd say that scrub dog of his was snoopin' around."

Scrub spent another night on the cabin porch. In the morning he toured about the place once more. There had never been a sound of movement. He could find no scent that he associated with people living here. This was the right place, yet it was completely strange. There was nothing here to hold him. He trotted across the clearing, stopped at the edge of the woods, and looked back at the cabin. He barked once in a forlorn sort of hope, then turned, and disappeared among the trees. He was going to the only friend he had left. He was going back to Scotty.

- 13 -

David watched the Anchorage paper during the Fairbanks North American race for some word of Smiley Jackson and Scrub. He saw the list of race entries, but Jackson was not among them. He wondered where the musher had gone and what had happened to Scrub. Jackson was mad enough that last day at Anchorage to kill the dog. David was sure that Jackson was broke. The few minor races he'd won didn't bring in enough prize money to support a team until next winter. He guessed Jackson had sold the team rather than go to work to support them.

Whether Scrub was dead or alive, David feared he was gone forever. He put the little ivory dog in the top dresser drawer. But he couldn't forget Scrub.

Nothing had changed for David. His aunt treated him well and never showed favoritism. His Uncle George was fine. But he was usually home only evenings and no special bond developed between them. Terry paid scant attention to David. He skated nightly on the ice pond at his friend's home. After that first time David never stopped again. Terry would speak briefly and even talk at home, or if they met on the street and David was alone. He barely said "hello" if he was with his friends.

After dinner at home, Terry generally headed for his room to do homework. Sometimes he went to the home of one of his friends.

Grace was the one warm, friendly person David felt close to. Her friendship helped fill the void created by the loss of his parents and Scrub. He met her every night at the bus stop, and they walked home together. He still helped her with math when she needed it. On Saturdays David took her exploring. He showed her parts of the city that, as a girl alone, she would never have seen. They were watching a freighter loading at the dock one day and Grace said, "I never would have seen a big ship like this if you hadn't come. Mom's afraid for me to come down here alone and Terry won't bring me."

When they hiked out of the city, Aunt Margaret cautioned, "You both be careful. There's moose around, you know."

They saw several moose in the distance, but David steered well away from them. Grace had never seen a rabbit run. She knew nothing about setting a snare or a deadfall. He showed her where a weasel had chased and caught a rabbit. He explained how grouse burrowed under the snow to escape storms and that sometimes a crust formed on top, trapping them.

"Gee, Davie," she said, "you know a lot."

"Dad knew more," he said. "All trappers have to know these things."

David was acquainted with every street in the city and now some of the businessmen spoke to him. He got more snow-shoveling jobs and he was often hired for a few hours to help uncrate merchandise or clean up a storeroom. The money he made was added to the roll in the toe of his mukluk. He had a hundred and forty dollars now.

David often worked in the hardware store. Several times when he was there Terry stopped to look at the shotgun in the window. But if David went toward the front of the store, Terry turned away.

David was surprised when he climbed the stairs one Saturday and found Terry standing in the middle of his room, looking around.

Startled, Terry stammered, "I—I thought I heard you up here."

"I just got home."

Terry crushed the cap in his hands and looked about, "You've got it pretty nice up here." He glanced out the window. "You can see almost all the way downtown."

"Didn't you ever come up here before?" David asked.

"What's that mean? I told you, I thought I heard you up here."

"I mean before I came?" David asked.

Terry shook his head and muttered, "Maybe once

178

or twice. Guess I never bothered to look out the window."

David sat on the bed and waited. Terry seemed nervous and ill at ease.

"Uh, Dave, how'd you like to go on a rabbit hunt some Saturday?"

"I don't have a gun. I guess mine's at Scotty's now."

"Uh, I'll borrow Dad's shotgun. We can take turns. Rabbits will be good only a couple of weeks longer. Spring's coming."

"I'd like it fine," David said. "When do we go?"

"I'll let you know." Terry hurried back down the stairs.

So Terry had finally decided to become friends and found it embarrassing, David thought. He was glad his cousin had come up to his room.

Two weeks went by and Terry said no more about the hunt.

David reminded him, "If we don't go on that rabbit hunt soon, it'll be too late. It almost is now."

"What?" Terry said. "Oh, yeah, the rabbit hunt. I guess it's off." He gave no further explanation.

Warm winds blew over Anchorage. The snow in the streets began to thaw. Water ran in the gutters. Those who'd been wearing parkas and mukluks put them away for thinner clothing.

Mr. Andrews at the hardware store hired David to help put away the winter ski and other sports equipment. He didn't finish that day. Mr. Andrews gave him five dollars and said, "Come back in the morning, Dave. We've got about half a day's work yet."

That night when David went to add the five dollars to the rest in his mukluk, there was no roll of bills in the toe. He checked the other mukluk. The money was not there either.

He sat on the bed and tried to think. He remembered having put another five dollars away just a week ago. He'd counted his money a number of times, but he always returned it to the mukluk. To make sure he hadn't misplaced it, he searched the room. He went into every dresser drawer, looked under the mattress, the pillow, in the pockets of his spare clothing. He found nothing.

He wondered about rats or mice. Pack rats would carry off things. But he hadn't seen a rat or any sign of one. And he'd heard no sounds to indicate they were about. Mystified, David finally went to bed, but he couldn't sleep for thinking about it.

He was still worried next morning, and his aunt asked, "Is anything wrong, David?"

"No," he said uncertainly.

"Maybe you're sick," Grace offered solicitously.

"For gosh sakes," Terry said, "Dave looks all right."

When Terry and Grace left for school, David returned to his room for another quick look in daylight. Maybe he'd missed some place. He found nothing, and finally left for work at the hardware store.

He finished the job in the early afternoon and Mr. Andrews paid him.

As David started to leave he glanced in the big display window. Something was different. He looked the window over carefully. The little shotgun was gone.

He pointed at the spot and asked Mr. Andrews, "What happened to the shotgun?"

"Sold it the other day. Thought I never would. It was pretty small. I was about to give up on it when this kid walked in and bought it."

"A kid?" David asked.

"About your age. It was really a kid's gun, too light for a man."

David went down the street. He reached the corner and waited for the light to change. Then it came to him.

At first he was a little sick, then angry. He glanced in a jewelry-store window at a clock. Grace would be getting off the bus in another half hour. He didn't want to meet her today.

David turned off the main street and headed toward home. He walked six blocks, then entered a small grove of trees and sat down on a stump. In a few minutes Grace came by, swinging her books and looking about for him. She disappeared around the corner. Some minutes later Terry and his three friends wandered down the street. They stopped in front of the house where they'd skated all winter and talked. Then Terry hurried off alone. He returned carrying a gun. The four boys went to the end of the street and out across the open country. David followed far behind.

The boys finally stopped and began tossing cans and bottles into the air. They took turns shooting at them.

David returned to the grove of trees and sat down to wait. It was almost dark when the boys came back. They split up in front of the house and Terry went down the street with the gun. David followed. Finally, a block from home, Terry turned onto a vacant lot. David ducked behind a bush and watched.

Terry went to the back of the lot to a little deserted cabin. He stopped at the door, looked all about, then ducked inside.

David ran noiselessly for the cabin. When he burst through the door, Terry had wrapped gunnysacks around the gun and was in the act of hiding it under a pile of old rags. Terry stared at David, mouth open in shocked surprise.

David pointed at the gun and said angrily, "So that's where my money went. You sneaked up to my room and stole it and bought that gun."

Terry found his voice then. "You're a liar!" he shouted.

"You were looking for my money the night I came home and caught you," David went on. "You figured to steal it then. But I came home too soon. That invitation to go rabbit hunting was the only excuse you could think up in a hurry."

"That's a lie!" Terry yelled.

David advanced, fists clenched. "I had almost a hundred and sixty dollars in that mukluk. Where's the rest of it?"

"I don't know anything about your old money." Terry began backing away.

David hit him and Terry's head cracked back against the logs. He hit him again. "Where's that money?"

Terry dropped the gun, ducked his head, and charged into David. Both boys went down in a tangle of arms and legs. They were almost matched for size and strength, but David was fighting mad. He rolled on top of Terry, pinned him to the floor, and began banging his head up and down, demanding, "Where's my money? Where is it?"

Terry tried to roll him off, but he was pinned solid and helpless. David's savage anger and the fierce head pounding frightened Terry. He cried, "In my pocket. In my pocket."

David ripped the handful of bills from Terry's pocket, but in doing so lost his pinning hold. Terry rolled him off, jumped to his feet, and dashed out the door.

David rushed after him, stuffing the money in his pocket. Terry charged blindly across the vacant lot for home with David tight to his heels. Neither boy saw the car coming until they were right on it.

Brakes squealed, the car door opened, and Uncle George stepped out. Both boys pulled up panting. Uncle George looked sharply at Terry, saw his scratched face, bloody mouth, and eye that was beginning to puff. He looked at David and asked very quietly, "What goes on here?"

David panted, "He sneaked into my room and stole the money I'd been saving and bought a gun. It's over there in that old cabin."

183

Terry wiped a smear of blood from his mouth with the back of his hand and said, "He's lying, Pa."

Uncle George looked at Terry, "Is there a gun in that cabin?"

Terry nodded, "I—I bought it with my own money."

"Get it," Uncle George said.

"Pa! I did buy it. It's mine."

"Get it!" Uncle George repeated.

Terry returned to the cabin and got the gun.

"Now both of you get in the car," Uncle George said. "We're going home."

Aunt Margaret looked at Terry's face when they entered the kitchen and said, "Good heavens, Terry! Whatever happened?"

Uncle George said, "Wash up, Terry. Then come into the living room."

"George," Aunt Margaret demanded. "What happened? Whose gun is that?"

"We'll get those answers in a minute," Uncle George said grimly.

In the living room David sat tensely on the edge of a chair. His aunt and Grace sat on the davenport. Terry sat on another chair dabbing with a towel at his swollen lips. Uncle George stood.

"Now then," he looked at David, "you say Terry stole the money you'd been saving and bought this gun. How do you know that?"

"After I gave you and Aunt Margaret two hundred and fifty dollars and bought my clothes, I had a hundred and four dollars left. I hid ninety in my mukluk and kept fourteen in my purse. I made some money shoveling snow and working in stores cleaning up and things. I put that in the mukluk with the rest. That money's gone and Terry's got the gun. I came home a couple of weeks ago and caught him in my room looking around."

"I went up to invite you on a rabbit hunt," Terry said angrily.

"That we never went on." David looked at his uncle. "He had the rest of the money in his pocket. I took it away from him in that old cabin."

"You're a liar," Terry shouted. "I earned that gun."

"David!" his aunt said shocked, "you're calling Terry a thief."

"I'm sorry," David said.

Uncle George held up a hand. "How much did you have in the mukluk, David?"

"About a hundred and sixty dollars."

"You say you took the rest away from Terry. How much have you now?"

"I don't know." David pulled the wad of bills from his pocket and handed them to his uncle. "The gun cost seventy-eight dollars."

"That's all he ever had," Terry shouted. "He's had it in his own pocket all the time. He's making this whole thing up, Pa."

"Be quiet." Uncle George calmly counted the money and laid it on the table. "Seventy-nine dollars," he said.

"He bought a box of shells," David said.

Uncle George looked at Terry. "All right, now let's have your side of it."

"I earned that money," Terry said angrily, "no matter what he says."

"How did you earn it?"

"How? Why—why, I worked, Pa."

"What did you work at?"

"Gee, Pa, the same things Dave did."

"I know about David's work. Tell me about yours."

"Well— I saw Dave working around shoveling snow and things, and I did it, too. I saved the money and bought that gun. I've been wanting it for months."

"Why didn't you bring it home?"

"You'd have taken it away from me. You said I was too young for a gun. Remember?"

"And I meant it. Go on."

"That's all, Pa. I earned the money working around after school at stores and places."

"You went ice skating every night with your friends over at Dolan's," David said. "I saw you."

"You saw me a few times," Terry said. "Not every night. That money right there is all you've ever had." He turned to his father. "He wanted that gun, too, Pa. He was mad because I got it, and he followed me in that old cabin and started beating me up."

"You did that to Terry's face!" Aunt Margaret said, shocked. "I'm not going to sit here and have my son made out a thief and liar and then beaten up by some half-breed Indian."

"Margaret!" Uncle George said sharply, "we'll have no more of that."

"Well, it's true," her blue eyes snapped. "He is a half-breed and you're standing there letting him call your son a liar and thief and doing nothing about it."

"David happens to be my brother's son," Uncle George said flatly. "He's as welcome here as any niece or nephew of either of us. Certainly David's half-Indian, but I'm not going to have that word thrown around here as if it was something to be ashamed of. There are a few things you'd better start learning if you expect to live up here."

"There are some things I'll never learn," Aunt Margaret said in a level voice. "You may as well know it now, George."

David felt sick. He thought his aunt was used to the fact he was half-Indian. Now he knew she'd been hiding her feelings until this moment. The family was quarreling over him. If only he hadn't lost his temper when he saw Terry with the gun. He said to his uncle, "Terry can have the gun."

His uncle handed him his money. "That's not the point, David. Tomorrow morning we're going downtown and settle this. Do you remember the places you worked?"

"Yes," David said, "all of them."

"We'll check them out to make sure you're telling the truth." He turned to Terry. "You said you worked. We'll check out yours, too."

"You're taking David's word for this," Aunt Margaret said angrily. "You're condemning your own son."

"I'm condemning no one," Uncle George said. "I'm getting to the bottom of this. One of those stories won't hold up."

"I can't remember all the places I worked," Terry complained.

"Why? David can."

"Dave had nothing else to do all day, so he remembers," Terry said. "I went to school and worked nights and Saturdays."

"You better remember enough to make the price of this gun," Uncle George said.

Aunt Margaret bit her lip. "You're taking sides. Don't deny it."

Uncle George nodded. "The side of the one telling the truth. We'll learn who that is tomorrow morning. Is dinner ready, Margaret?"

Aunt Margaret started to say something. Then she rose abruptly and went into the kitchen.

Terry followed her.

Grace still sat on the davenport. She looked like she was going to cry.

"Out! and wash up, honey," Uncle George said. "Dinner'll be ready soon."

Grace left without a word.

"Come on, David."

David shook his head. He couldn't sit at the table and eat with them now. "I can't," he said.

Uncle George nodded. "I understand. I'm sorry about this, David."

David climbed the stairs to his room. He closed the door, lay full-length on the bed, and stared out the window. The lights of the city had come on and threw a high fan into the dark sky. Headlights intermittently probed the street. It was quieter downstairs than usual. Occasionally a voice funneled up the stairwell. The anger and shock of this evening depressed them all.

An hour or so later Uncle George climbed the stairs and entered the room. He stood tall and lean in the dark and looked down at the boy. He reminded David more than ever of his father. "Not hungry yet?" he asked gently.

"No."

His uncle sat in the chair at the head of the bed. "If you get hungry during the night, go downstairs and raid the refrigerator. Hear?"

"Yes."

"About your aunt. She didn't mean to sound as severe as she did. She's been in Alaska less than two years and the change has been pretty rough on her. She's got a lot to learn about the north. We have to give her more time. She'll come around."

"I wish I'd kept my mouth shut," David burst out. "Terry can have the gun. I don't want it."

"As I said before, that's not the point. If Terry took your money, I want to know it. He'll earn it somehow and pay back every dime. We'll straighten this out in the morning and everything will be all right. It's not a tragedy, just a problem. Families have them all the time. We had some pretty serious ones long before you came. I just want you to know that and not worry." He stood up to go.

"You're a lot like Dad," David said.

"We had the same parents you know." He tousled David's hair. "Remember, this is your home every bit as much as it is Grace and Terry's." He opened the door. "If you get hungry, go down and eat. Hear?"

"Yes," David said, "and thanks, Uncle George."

David listened to his uncle's feet going downstairs. Maybe they'd get everything straightened out tomorrow, but it would never be all right again. His aunt wasn't going to change the way she felt about him. Terry didn't like him, and now David admitted it was mutual. Grace and his uncle were the only ones who cared about him. His presence split the family. He had never belonged and he never could. He could not stay here any longer.

He began thinking of Aurora, his old home, the trap line, and Scotty. He thought of Noble and the dog team. The Moores had said he could have them any time he came back. He belonged back in Aurora, in his own home, doing what he knew best, hiking the mountains and tundra he'd always known.

David rose and cracked the door open slightly to hear the sounds below. Then he went back and lay down and waited. Gradually the house quieted down. He closed his door and began to gather up the few belongings he'd brought. He stuffed them into the old knapsack. When he finished, he stood looking about the room.

Then he remembered the little ivory dog and took it from the dresser drawer. A wave of loneliness went through him as he thought of all the things Scrub and he had done together.

David found a piece of paper and studied over leaving a note. Finally he wrote: *I'm sorry for everything. I'm going where I belong—to my mother's people. I know where they are. Please don't try to find me. I'll be fine. Thanks for keeping me.*

He opened the door carefully and listened. All was quiet and dark downstairs. But still he waited. The clock chimed the half hour, then the hour. He counted twelve. Carrying the knapsack, he went carefully down the stairs. At the foot he turned into the hall, passed his aunt and uncle's door, then Terry's, and came to Grace's. He eased it open and stepped inside. David leaned over the bed and placed his hand over Grace's mouth. Her eyes flew open.

"Be quiet," he whispered.

She sat bolt upright and whispered, "Davie! what're you doing?"

"Leaving," he said.

"You can't," she whispered.

"Yes, I can."

"Don't, Davie," she begged. "Everything will be all right. Wait till after tomorrow. Dad'll make Terry pay you back, every cent. I know Terry took your money. I saw him skating almost every night. He didn't work anyplace. I couldn't say it down there, but I will now if it'll help."

David shook his head. "I never should have come here," he whispered. "I don't belong."

"Wait and let Dad take care of it. Please."

"When Uncle George finds out tomorrow, it'll just make everything worse. I came to tell you good-bye and give you this." He handed her the little ivory dog.

She held it in her hands. "It's Scrub," she whispered. "I'll always keep it, Davie. Always." She looked up, her eyes big and round in the room's dark. "Where'll you go?"

"I left a note in my room," David said. "I—I'm going to my mother's folks."

"Do you know where they are?"

"Yes," he said, "but it's better if I don't tell you."

"You don't want Dad to find you," she said. "How will you go to them, Davie?"

"I—I met some people down at the docks. I'll go by boat."

Tears glistened in Grace's eyes. "I'll never see you again, will I?"

"You can remember me with the dog."

"I'll never forget you," she whispered. "Never." She put her arms around his neck and kissed him. "I wish you wouldn't go."

"I have to." He picked up the knapsack. "Good-bye." He stepped back into the hall and closed the door softly.

A minute later he was outside, hurrying down the street toward the city. He had lied in the note he'd left and he had lied to Grace. He meant to catch the late-night bus heading up the highway toward Fairbanks. He knew exactly where he'd get off. By the time they missed him in the morning he'd be off the bus, hiking out across the rolling tundra. He'd be on his way home to Aurora.

- 14 -

Scotty was not surprised that Scrub had left. It was logical the dog might head back for Aurora to look for David. What amazed him was that he had tried so soon, as stiff and battered as he seemed to be. He doubted the dog would get far, so he spent half the day searching the brush and tundra for several miles in the direction of Aurora. He expected to find Scrub lying somewhere, exhausted. There was no sign of him. He wondered what the dog would do when he found no one at David's old home. He might go wild. He looked enough like a wolf to join a pack. Scotty hoped Scrub would return to him. If he didn't, he decided, he'd get another pup. With Fred, Celia, and David gone and no one to visit once in a while, he needed some kind of company.

Scotty spent the rest of the day repairing the riffles in his sluice boxes. The next morning he got his boat into the river and loaded the sluice boxes. The powerful outboard motor ferried them the half mile up-river to the little feeder stream he planned to work. It took the rest of the day to set the boxes. The following morning he began prospecting the creek bottom. By noon he knew it was worth working, but it was not rich.

Scotty hiked back to the cabin for lunch. He was about to enter, when Smiley Jackson stepped from the nearby trees and came toward him. Scotty asked, "What brings you here, Smiley?"

"Goin' home," Jackson said. "Racin' season's over."

"How'd you do?"

Jackson shrugged, "Won some and lost some. Got a good price for the team, so I sold it. I'll get a better one for next year."

Same old Smiley Jackson, Scotty thought. "Come in, I'll put the coffeepot on." The courtesy of the trail could not be denied.

Jackson followed Scotty inside, slipped the pack from his back, and sat down. He looked about the cabin while Scotty lit the stove and began getting lunch. It was the first time he'd ever been inside Scotty's place. There was a whip hanging on the wall, and Jackson asked, "You wanta sell that? I lost mine."

Scotty shook his head. "It's sort of a keepsake now."

The door to the back room was open and Jackson saw a large pile of furs. "I thought you quit trappin' years ago when you lost your hand."

"I did."

"What's all the fur doin' here?" Jackson rose and walked into the back room.

Scotty frowned. Living alone he paid little attention

whether doors were open or closed, whether things were in sight or not. "That fur belongs to Davie Martin," he said. "It's what him and his pa caught before the accident. Fur buyer will be coming in about three days and I'll sell it for Davie."

"I remember hearin' his folks froze to death." Jackson ran a hand over several pelts. "Nice-lookin' fur. They was havin' a mighty good year. There must be seven or eight thousand dollars' worth here."

Scotty kept his eyes on the frying pans, where potatoes and caribou steaks were frying. There was no use denying it. Jackson knew the value of fur. "Could be," he said. "Depends on the price this year."

"Oh, sure." Jackson came back into the kitchen and sat down.

They ate in almost complete silence. Scotty asked once, "Whatever happened to that big leader you had?"

"Scrub? I told you I sold the team."

Scotty nodded. "Saw him once. I thought he had the makings of a good leader."

"Did have, but Fred Martin's kid spoiled 'im."

"How?" Scotty asked.

"Made a pet of 'im. Can't do that with a sled dog. It ruins 'em." Jackson's eyes strayed to the open door of the back room. "That fur buyer comin' right up here to the cabin?"

"Frank Weathers has floats on his plane. Ice is gone outa the river, so he'll land and run right up to the bank."

196

Jackson nodded. "That fur's as nice as I've ever seen. It'll bring top dollar."

"Could be," Scotty agreed.

"You're sellin' it for the kid?"

Scotty nodded. He'd never known Jackson to talk so much. "Weathers will pick up the fur here. We'll settle on a price, and he'll deliver the money to Davie in Anchorage."

"The kid ever comin' back?"

"I don't think so. He's living with his dad's relatives."

Jackson finished his lunch in silence, then rose, and slipped on the pack. "Gotta get movin'. Wanta make home by tomorra night." His eyes went to the back room again, "Lotta money for a kid to be gettin'," he observed.

"Davie and his uncle will find a use for it," Scotty said.

Jackson shook his head. "Too much for any kid. Just too much. What's a kid know 'bout money?" He nodded to Scotty by way of thanks and left.

Scotty watched him go off down-river and disappear in the brush. Then he cleaned up the lunch dishes, took up the rifle, and hiked off up-river to his sluice boxes. He was glad Smiley Jackson was gone.

Jackson did not go far. He couldn't get the picture of that pile of fur out of his mind. He sat on a stump and thought about it. There was a lot of money represented there. More than the first prize of the Fur Rendezvous or the North American. Maybe twice as much as he'd got for selling the team. More than enough to take care of all his problems, he thought greedily. With that much money he could buy a new team. One already trained and ready to run. And there'd be more than enough left to keep them in style until next winter's racing season. This time he wouldn't have to start with a bunch of unruly pups that he'd raised himself, spend months culling and trying to build them into a team. He wouldn't have to worry about a sponsor to help pay entry fees and feed bills. There might even be enough left over to get a truck to carry the dogs and sled around in.

All that money was going to a kid. The kid who'd ruined his lead dog, who'd caused him to lose the prize money and honor of winning the Fur Rendezvous. That Martin kid should have to repay him for his losses. It'd be a way to get revenge on the kid, he thought angrily.

Jackson went quietly back through the trees to where he could watch Scotty's cabin. He saw Scotty leave and head up-river, carrying the rifle. He waited another half hour. Then, convinced Scotty would remain working at his sluice boxes the rest of the afternoon, he went to the cabin.

The door was unlocked and Jackson walked in. He stood looking at the pile of furs, his mind busy. He could load the fur into Scotty's boat. Current and motor combined would take him flying down-river.

198

He'd be seventy or eighty miles away by the time Scotty returned.

But wouldn't Scotty immediately miss the furs and his boat, and guess who'd taken them?

Jackson was worrying about that when he became aware of two things—a red gasoline can in the corner, and that the cabin was unusually hot. He lifted a stove lid and looked into the firebox. Scotty hadn't doused the fire when he left. Then he had it. The stove and the gas can were the answers. He was surprised at how simple and foolproof it would be.

He'd load the fur into the boat, then scatter gas over the floor, and set fire to the cabin. When Scotty returned, he'd find nothing but a heap of smoldering ashes. Scotty would jump to the logical conclusion that he'd left a fire in the stove and that somehow it had spread to the cabin.

The missing boat was the only thing that worried Jackson. Scotty would have to think that the boat had broken loose in the fast current and drifted away. He couldn't prove otherwise.

Jackson knew a man about a hundred miles downriver who'd buy the fur and ask no questions. For a little extra he'd keep his mouth shut. By this time tomorrow he'd have the fur sold and the boat sunk in some deep hole where there'd be no trace.

Jackson got to work immediately. He made the fur into bales and began carrying them to the boat.

He was returning from the first trip, when he thought

199

he glimpsed a gray animal watching him from the brush. It faded from sight and he wasn't sure he'd seen anything. Two more trips took all the fur. He was going to the cabin for the last time, when he caught a definite movement in the brush. Jackson walked over to the spot, but saw nothing. To have any eyes watching gave him an uncomfortable feeling. If he had a rifle, he'd hunt the animal down.

In the cabin Jackson filled the stove with wood and opened the draft to get the fire roaring. Next he scattered gas about the floor. He was reaching for the bottle of matches on a shelf above the window, when he glanced outside.

Scotty was walking toward the cabin. Jackson looked about frantically for a weapon. Scotty's old whip with its long hard handle was the only one he saw. He snatched it down and stepped to one side of the door.

Scotty swung the door open, went straight to the stove, and lifted one of the lids. He was looking into the firebox when Jackson brought the butt of the whip down on his head. Scotty collapsed and lay still.

Jackson found rope and bound Scotty tight to a chair before he regained consciousness.

Scotty groaned and straightened. He blinked his eyes and shook his head, to clear it. He strained on the ropes binding his arms and legs to the chair. They were very tight. Then he looked up at Jackson.

"Why'd you come back, you crazy fool?" Jackson demanded.

"I got to thinkin' of that pile of fur and the way you talked. I wanted to make sure you'd left. I should've been careful comin' in." Scotty sniffed. "Gasoline! You were going to burn my cabin down. What'd you do with the furs?" He twisted his head around, trying to look into the back room.

"You should have stayed up there shovelin' gravel," Jackson said bitterly.

Scotty looked at him steadily. "What'll you do now?"

Jackson scowled. The scar on his cheek was an angry streak. He'd come this far. He meant to have the money those furs would bring. He thought briefly of leaving Scotty tied to the chair and setting fire to the cabin. The binding ropes would burn off. Scotty would be found dead, probably by the pilot due here three days from now. It would still look like an accident that had trapped Scotty.

He discarded that idea. Murder was not part of Jackson's makeup. Besides, the police never stopped looking for a murderer. There had to be another way.

"You got a problem," Scotty said. "A real problem."

Jackson ignored him and kept thinking of his original plan. It could still work. Just before taking off, he'd loosen Scotty's bonds enough so he could free himself in time. With only one hand, that would be a very slow job. Scotty would have to hike to Aurora thirty miles away to call the police by shortwave. It would be about three days before they came. He'd be long gone. Scotty couldn't prove a thing against him. His story would mean nothing without proof. But it would be healthier to get out of the country for a while. There was a lot he could do with that much money.

"Got it all figured out, eh?" Scotty said. "You really think you can get away with it?"

"Shut up."

"I always knew you were dumb," Scotty said. "I didn't know you were a fool, too."

"We'll see." Jackson laid the rifle on the table and bent to loosen Scotty's bonds. He saw Scotty's eyes flick to the door, the look of surprise that widened them.

Jackson turned his head quickly. A big wolf-gray animal stood just outside the open door. His head was tipped down slightly, his amber eyes slanted upward, studying Jackson.

Scrub!

Jackson could hardly believe it. Scrub should have got hung up with that chain around his neck and starved to death days ago. All the trouble he'd had the past year could be traced to this dog. Jackson grabbed for the rifle.

Scrub was gone in an instant.

Jackson rushed outside, slamming the door. There was no dog. He dashed around the cabin in time to glimpse the wolfish shape fade into the trees. He waited, hoping Scrub would show himself. Minutes passed. Jackson wanted to hunt the dog down and kill him. But he didn't dare take the time. He had to get away from here. He waited a few more minutes, then returned to the front of the cabin.

Jackson was about to open the door, when a figure with a pack on its back emerged from the trees. With a shock, Jackson recognized David Martin. He glanced toward the boat. It was in plain sight to the boy. The fur was visible.

Jackson went to meet David. He approached at an angle that made the boy turn his back on the boat to face him.

"What're you doin' here, kid?" Jackson asked.

"I stopped to see Scotty." David seemed as surprised and uncomfortable as Jackson.

"Scotty said you was livin' in Anchorage with relatives." The man's lips twitched nervously in the permanent smile. His eyes never quite met David's.

"I'm going home."

"To Aurora! You gonna live there alone?"

"Yes." David glanced about. Why was Jackson here? Why was he walking around Scotty's, carrying a rifle as if he'd been hunting?

"Dontcha like the big city?"

"Aurora's home." Jackson had never talked to him before. Why was he now? "Where's Scotty?"

"Checkin' his sluice boxes. He's got 'em in a creek about half a mile up-river."

David wanted to ask about Scrub, but he was afraid of touching off Jackson's hair-trigger temper. He asked, "Are you heading for Aurora?"

Jackson nodded. "Had a cup of coffee with Scotty. I'm leavin' now."

David stepped beyond Jackson and glanced about,

puzzled. Then he saw the boat pulled up against the bank, the pile of furs inside. Jackson said, "Scotty's takin' it down-river to some fur buyer."

There was something here David didn't understand. "I'd almost forgot," he said. "Scotty did say he'd sell it for me. Guess I won't wait. I'll see him later." David headed up past the cabin, Jackson trailing him closely. As he came opposite the cabin, he noticed smoke pouring from the stovepipe. He turned quickly, stepped to the cabin, and threw open the door.

Scotty looked up from where he sat bound to the chair. "Davie!" he said, "what're you doing here?"

The rifle muzzle jammed hard into David's back, and Jackson said, "Welcome to the party."

Scotty said, "Davie, you shouldn't have come."

"I knew something was wrong when I saw the fur in the boat and smoke coming from the stovepipe," David said.

"Nothin' wrong," Jackson said. "You're payin' back what you made me lose at the Fur Rendezvous."

"That's no excuse for tying up Scotty like this."

"It is now."

"You must be crazy," David said.

"Then you'd better face against that wall and put your hands behind your back like I say." Jackson reached for a length of rope.

Scotty yanked at his bonds. "What're you going to do to him?"

"Same thing I did to you."

204

"You'll never get away with it. Best thing you can do is turn us loose and get outa here."

"Too late for that," Jackson said. "Get against that wall, kid."

David backed up, eyes darting about for some kind of weapon. There was nothing but a butcher knife on the table. There was movement at the door behind Jackson.

A gray, wolflike animal was looking in. His amber eyes sprung wide open as he looked at David. His bushy tail began to whip and his mouth opened wide in a dog-like grin. The sight of the dog he thought he'd never see again so startled David that he yelled, "Scrub!"

Jackson yanked the rifle around. David dived for the barrel, got hold of it, and tried to wrench it away. Jackson let go with one hand and drove his fist into David's face. David fell, still clutching the barrel. Jackson struck and yanked, and struck again. The rifle was torn from the boy's hands.

David was trying to get to his knees, when Scrub launched himself through the door with a snarl of rage. He drove straight for Jackson's throat. His big teeth missed and clamped down on the forearm thrown up to ward him off. He ripped through cloth and into the arm.

Jackson stumbled back with a cry of fright and pain. The rifle clattered to the floor. The dog's driving weight threw Jackson off balance and he fell on his back Scrub was on him, snarling horribly, razor-sharp teeth slashed at the arms the man threw over his face to protect himself.

David snatched up the rifle and jumped to his feet.

Scotty tore at his bonds, yelling, "Cut me loose, Davie! Cut me loose!"

David grabbed the butcher knife and severed the ropes.

Jackson fought off Scrub and got to his feet. He aimed a wild kick at the dog, then ran blindly for the door. Scrub leaped again. Jackson stumbled against the table and went to his knees. He let out a bawl of fright and grabbed for the raging dog to hold him off. Scrub's teeth sank into his hand. Then the dog was all over him. It was as if he were paying Jackson back for the beatings the man had given him during the winter.

Scrub was a slashing, ripping demon. The cabin was an uproar of snarls, growls, and Jackson's yells. Every time the man struck or tried to shove the dog off, he exposed his face and throat and those snapping teeth were right after him. Finally Jackson doubled himself into a knot on the floor, arms wrapped about his face and neck, and yelled in terror, "Get 'im off me! Get 'im off me!"

The sound of his nasal voice infuriated the dog more. He tore at the protecting arms. His flashing teeth shredded Jackson's coat and shirt.

Scotty threw off the last of the ropes, grabbed the rifle from David, and said, "Pull off your dog before he kills Jackson."

David got his arms around Scrub's neck and dragged

206

him off. The dog kept growling, snarling, and lunging against David's arms, trying to break free. David said sharply, "Cut that out! Stop it! Hear!" He cuffed Scrub's ears and the snarling gradually sank to a growl, but the dog never took his eyes from Jackson.

Scotty said, "You can get up now."

Jackson got shakily to his feet and collapsed on the bench, arms hanging at his sides. Both arms and his left hand were torn and bleeding. The front of his shirt was ripped away, and two big teeth marks showed how close Scrub had come to his throat. Jackson looked at Scrub as if he'd never seen the dog before. He kept muttering, "Hang onto 'im! Keep 'im off me! Keep 'im off! He's gone mad."

Scrub's amber eyes were fixed on Jackson with almost human hate and the growl rumbling from his chest never stopped.

David asked, "What do we do now?"

"First off," Scotty said, "we'd better patch him up. Put Scrub in the other room."

David shoved the growling Scrub into the back room and closed the door. Scrub scratched and growled.

Scotty handed David the rifle. "Just in case he gets ideas." Then he went to work on Jackson's arms and hand with disinfectants and bandages. The only sounds were Scrub's growling and scratching.

Scotty finally finished and said, "All right. Now get out!"

"No!" David said. "We're taking him to Aurora and calling the police."

"We can do that," Scotty agreed, "and we can have him put in jail for some time. There'll be a trial, and we'll have to go to Anchorage to testify against him. That could take weeks and be a lot of inconvenience and trouble. I don't think he's worth it."

"So he gets off scot-free?" David said angrily.

"No such thing." Scotty fixed Jackson with a tough look. "I figure to let you go, but if you're smart, you'll get out of this part of the country fast. I'm going to swear out a warrant for your arrest the first time I get to a shortwave station and can call the police. That warrant's going to hang over your head from now on. If you ever show up around here again, the police will be notified and you'll be arrested. Then Davie and I will take the time to go in and testify against you. Now take your pack and get outa here."

Jackson stood up uncertainly. "That dog in there's mine."

"He don't sound like yours," Scotty said.

"Still mine."

"He stays here," David said.

"He's legally mine."

"We're buying him from you," Scotty said. "Davie, get a pencil and paper and write what I say."

David found pencil and paper and Scotty dictated: *"For the sum of one dollar I have sold to David Martin one wolf-gray dog that answers to the name of Scrub.* Put down the date. Smiley, sign it. Davie, give him a dollar."

208

"He's a lead dog," Jackson said angrily. "He's worth a thousand."

"A dollar," Scotty said. "Take it or leave it. But if you leave it, you go in that room alone and take him out."

"That's how you figure to get back at me," Jackson said. "Cheatin' me outa my dog."

"A dollar," Scotty repeated, "or you go in there and get him."

Jackson looked at the closed door behind which Scrub growled and scratched. He swallowed nervously. Then he laboriously signed his name and started to go out.

"Pick up your dollar," Scotty said sharply, "or this sale's not legal."

Jackson turned and glared at him. "Make up your mind," Scotty warned. "I'm not going to leave the dog in that room much longer."

Jackson picked up the dollar and stomped out.

David and Scotty followed. Jackson started down-river.

"Not that way," Scotty called.

"That's my home. Where else can I go?" Jackson yelled.

"It's a big country. Just remember to stay away from here."

Jackson looked about uncertainly, then he headed up-river, and disappeared in the trees.

"That's the last we'll ever see of him," Scotty said.

"Let your dog out before he wrecks the back room."

When David opened the door, Scrub tore out, ready to do battle to protect him.

David fell on his knees and began to shake the big head. "Smiley Jackson's gone forever," he laughed. "You're mine now. All mine. Quit acting so tough."

Scrub jumped on David then, whining and licking his face and barking wildly. Boy and dog rolled on the ground in a threshing bundle of arms and legs, barks and yells.

Scotty watched until they stopped.

"Now," he smiled, "let's get the fur back to the cabin and clean up the place."

Evening shadows had darkened the kitchen when they finished. David filled Scotty in on most of what had happened to him in Anchorage. Now he sat rubbing Scrub's head and said, "Scrub and I are going back to Aurora to live. We'll run the trap line."

"That's a long line for one man," Scotty reminded him. "Your dad was one of the best and you know how tough he found it."

"I've thought about that. I'd like to have a partner. But it'd have to be somebody I knew and could get along with." David kept rubbing the dog's head. "Scotty," he asked finally, "would you be interested in going partners with me?"

"Me?" Scotty asked, surprised.

"I've got an awful lot to learn, and you could teach me. I'd be another pair of hands to your one," David

210

said in a rush. "We could live in this cabin or—or mine."

"Yours would be better," Scotty said. "It's bigger, more centrally located, and there's that shed out back to keep the fur in."

"Gee!" David said. "Would you?"

"I've been wanting to get back for a long time," Scotty confessed. "There was just no good way before."

"Then you'll do it?"

"We could work the line like your dad did," Scotty said thoughtfully.

"Dad and Mom would sure like it if they knew," David said hopefully.

"I kinda think they would at that," Scotty agreed.

"Then it's a deal?"

"It's a deal."

They shook hands.

"Now that we've got our futures settled, how about something to eat?" Scotty asked. He stirred up the fire and got out a frying pan and mixing bowl. "I'd say this calls for a celebration and something special. What'll it be?"

"Anything you say," David smiled, knowing what was coming.

"Anybody for bacon pancakes?"

"That's fine."

Scotty looked at Scrub. "How about you, friend?"

David leaned over and rubbed his cheek against Scrub's furry forehead. "This's a special celebration for you, too," he said. "You got rid of Smiley Jackson forever today. So, what'll you have?"

Scrub lifted his lips in a grin and thumped his tail on the floor.

"We're all agreed," Scotty said, "bacon pancakes it is."

WALT MOREY was born in the heart of the Olympic Mountains in Hoquiam, Washington, and he spent his childhood in Montana, Canada, and Oregon. After his graduation from business college, Mr. Morey turned to writing and supported himself as a mill worker, construction worker, theater manager, and shipbuilder for the Kaiser Company. At the end of the Second World War, he went to Alaska as a diver and fish-trap inspector. His first children's book, *Gentle Ben*, received an ALA Notable Book Award and won the 1965 Dutton Junior Animal Book Award. It was also made into a movie and a national television series. Among his other titles are *North to Danger, Home Is the North, Gloomy Gus, Deep Trouble*, and *Kävik the Wolf Dog*, winner of the 1968 Dutton Junior Animal Book Award, the 1970 Dorothy Canfield Fisher Award, and the 1971 William Allen White Award. Mr. Morey and his wife now operate a sixty-acre filbert grove near Portland, Oregon.